AT THE SCENT OF WATER

Margaret Stewart

Margaret Stewart

PublishAmerica
Baltimore

At the specific preference of the author, PublishAmerica allowed this work to remain exactly as the author intended, verbatim, without editorial input.

ISBN: 1-4241-7285-3
PUBLISHED BY PUBLISHAMERICA, LLLP
www.publishamerica.com
Baltimore

Printed in the United States of America

AT THE SCENT OF WATER

Margaret Stewart

Chapter 1

When Marshal Enrique Sanchez thought back to the troubles that had sprung up at the Chuparrosa Town Hall meeting in late September, his clearest memory was of the little dog. Oh, sure, there'd been a dust-filled wind that night and a sweltering low-pressure system. There'd been two solid hours of slogging through the tension of angry Chuparrosa citizens screaming and shaking their fists at each other, but unpleasant hours like that were part of his job, and he trusted his skill at confrontations. He could put conflict in perspective and deal with the problems without emotion, without taking sides. Only later he cursed himself for that arrogance of mind. Dangerously later, after the revelation of the dog.

In the packed Chuparrosa council chamber on that September night, hisses of derision, like sparks from an ignited fuse, passed from mouth to mouth until they exploded in the front row. Sugar Morley, her startling turquoise eyes flashing out of a face screwed into a mask of scorn, jumped to her feet and began to shriek at the men huddled around the speaker's table.

"You lawless bastards! You're wrecking our way of life! Your goddamn grass is an insult on the face of our Sonoran Desert!"

Sanchez had been leaning against the back wall of the chamber, his arms folded, face impassive, while his eyes checked the bob of each head and the twitch of every shoulder. He could feel his own shoulders tighten against the sweat-soaked cloth of his uniform shirt. He was on duty, but hoping he wouldn't have to interfere in this community information session. Information session, hell! With tempers stressed to the limit, there were as many chances for trouble as there were bodies in the room.

Sugar's husband and their two ponderous sons, Jeremiah and Micah, rose to their feet, surrounding her with their presence, menacing and protective. The buzz behind them swelled to cheering, catcalls and raucous applause. Encouragement brought a glow to Sugar's face.

Off to one side, Sanchez saw Claire Tubbs, reporter for the Chuparrosa Hummer, leap to her feet and sprint up front, her camera poised for a better shot of the human wall of Morleys. The flash popped twice before she trotted back, looking as smug as a coyote after a rabbit dinner. Not much action in a small town like Chupparosa, Sanchez thought as he watched the triumphant Tubbs return to her seat. Summer was always a slow season. She hadn't covered a story as exciting as this since a grease fire blackened the kitchen of the Jimson Weed Saloon back in July.

Sanchez took a deep breath, sucking in the stuffy smell that filled the room. The angry speeches of the evening had removed most of the oxygen, leaving a warm, stagnant haze. Tonight the outdoor humidity was too high for the evaporative coolers to handle. The re-circulated, over-used air lay heavy with the fumes of conflict.

Outside it was even hotter, 98 degrees on this September evening in central Arizona, with matching humidity. The towering monsoon clouds, which had been piling up like meringue all day, now ringed the near mountains, their luminous depths convulsed from within by the fire bolts echoing off the mesas. Wind had moved in with the clouds, hot as a blast from hell and swirling with dust. The marshal could hear it moaning and whining as it bounced papery bougainvillea blossoms into the corners of the quadrangle enclosing the Town Hall plaza.

While the village of Chuparrosa waited breathlessly for rain, its angry residents in the city council chamber fought a bitter battle over water. So far the meeting was going badly for Chuparrosa's mayor and his cronies.

Mayor Mel Bergen banged his gavel as the mutterings of the crowd foamed toward him in resentful waves. He patted a folded handkerchief over his jowls and tugged at his shirt collar. Beside him at the long table, Roger Martineau, of Sonoran Skyline Residential Community, shuffled papers. A clap of thunder shuddered through the hall, and he leaned over, shielding his mouth with one hand, to whisper instructions in Bergen's ear.

"We have time for one more speaker from the citizen's water committee," the mayor shouted into his microphone, trying to be heard over the storms inside and out. His chin jutted as he consulted, through bifocals, the top card on the stack in front of him and raised his head, glowering at the audience. "Will Fiesta Flores come to the podium, please?"

Heads turned as people searched the room, worry and anticipation mingling in their faces. A young woman, her athletic body packed into white jeans and an orange tank top, moved with the grace of a lynx toward the mayor and reached for the mike. She spun on her toes, scanning the audience, her face calm, eyes alive, passionate. Her black hair, looped into coils at the back of her head, shimmered in the ceiling lights like skeins of silk. The edge of a violet hibiscus, plucked from the bush outside the Town Hall door, ruffled out in front of her left ear.

Sanchez pulled his shoulders off the wall and craned his neck with the rest of the crowd to get a better look. Fiesta was well worth looking at. He had seen her come in and been surprised that she would interest herself in the town's water problems. Not that she ever displayed a low profile, but her interests tended to be more exotic. Last week she was lobbying for permission to keep llamas and passing petitions to save endangered caribou herds in Alaska. Still, the five-acre spread, where she lived with her assorted livestock and Paseo horses, sat high on Spanish Saddle Mountain. To hear these folks talk, there wasn't any more water up there.

Fiesta gazed over the audience for a full dramatic moment. Hank grinned, appreciating her style and timing. Their eyes met for an instant, and he detected the slight lift of one sleek eyebrow in acknowledgment. She had made it plain, when he'd arrived from

7

Albuquerque fourteen months before to take the job of marshal in Chuparrosa, that he was welcome in her bed any time. He hadn't been interested in a casual love affair with a rich resident, so he'd made a bid for her friendship instead. It had become one of the soundest he had in this Anglo stronghold, and he valued her as a comrade bound by a common first language and traditions.

"Five years ago when I built my house, I had a well drilled." Fiesta's low voice, tinged with a lilt of its New Mexican roots, throbbed through the hall. "They struck water at ninety six feet and dug to a hundred eighty. With that I could provide for my horses and my pets, as well as for my own humble needs. There is not one blade of grass around my place. The desert landscaping survives on rain alone. I weep when the summer heat culls the weak plants, but here in Chuparrosa we understand the nature of the desert and the miracle that occurs when the rains come again."

Fiesta turned to nod to the perspiring gentlemen at the table. "Two years ago our friendly neighbor, Greenwood Development Corporation, began building Sonoran Skyline and watering their golf courses from the aquifer that also serves the wells on Spanish Saddle Mountain. That fall my well had to be drilled fifty feet deeper." She swept a look over the faces before her, gathering the power of their anger to herself.

"My story matches yours. Each fall my well has to be deepened. My well's volume is now totally undependable. Water barely dribbles out of the taps. So it is necessary to have water trucked in to fill the horse troughs and tanks. The experts tell us that the water level in the deep aquifer basin under Sonoran Skyline has dropped a hundred seventy feet since the golf course watering began!"

A shout came from one corner of the room. "*Vaya,* Fiesta!" She threw back her head with a smile that dissolved again in the seriousness of her subject.

"Those of us who live in this northernmost part of Chuparrosa are wholly dependent on the aquifer for our water supply. When our development was platted, we received a certificate from the state assuring us that there was enough for a hundred years. Enough for us and our children. We didn't know that this birthright would be bartered away to a higher bidder for a mess of commercial pottage!" The full, flame-colored lower lip in her tragic face quivered.

The crowd simmered in anticipation. Claire's camera flared again and again, recording the fiery orator and her listeners' antagonism.

"We cannot live in the desert without water. Our claim to the aquifer is that we were here first, and we were promised. We are not using exorbitant amounts of this sacred fluid to provide an environment that denies the desert, as is Sonoran Skyline Residential Development. We are simply trying to survive. We do not pour the precious liquid on the ground so that a few elite people can chose one of the three eighteen-hole golf courses on which they will play games. We are simply thirsty. Our needs are life and death needs." She raised clenched fists and whooped a battle cry. "While they play games, we are deadly serious!"

Sanchez glanced around, feeling the crowd rally to Fiesta with more spirit than they had to less inspired speakers. He moved along the wall to where his deputy, Kevin Dingle, stood with eyes fixed on the woman at the podium, his jaw slightly ajar.

"Watch this bunch," Hank murmured into Kevin's ear. "Fiesta would love to be the cause of a riot, so get ready to step in at the first sign of a disturbance."

The deputy shut his mouth and swung his earnest, freckled face toward the marshal. With the heel of his hand he brushed at the beads of sweat collecting on his eyebrows and nodded. "Yes sir."

Retracing his steps, Hank circled the outside of the crowd to a spot where he could watch the spectators' faces. The Mayor Bergen, Roger Martineau and Sonoran Skyline's lawyer had made presentations earlier in the long evening and fielded some questions. When members of the hastily formed water committee began hurling accusations at the three men, resentments on both sides blazed. A few handguns, standard equipment for several of the attending residents, had been checked at the door, but they lay on a back table within easy reach of these provoked citizens. If things got troublesome, Martineau and the mayor could be in danger.

"The Corporation is unpardonably insensitive to the desert environment," Fiesta raged into the mike. Her words pulsed through the hall like radar, bouncing off each upturned face. "The only god they honor is greed!"

Her eyes flashed signals around the room as cheering broke out. Spectators jumped to their feet with all the fervor of religious revivalists, hands flailing above their heads. A few in the back jumped on their chairs. The mayor hammered his gavel, attempting to get control once more.

"Thank you, Ms. Flores. Your time is up," he bellowed and stepped around the table to snatch back the microphone.

Fiesta gave him a radiant smile and stretched up on her toes to plant a kiss on his cheek. "Sure, Mel," she purred, cupping both hands around his as they held the mike. "We must take action to prevent this destruction of our community and our way of life. If the town won't help us, we must take matters into our own hands." Releasing the struggling mayor, she held her palms out to the audience in a gesture of appeal.

Another burst of cheering, gavel banging and camera flashing followed her as she danced back to her seat. There were smiles in the hall now, Hank noticed, and people nodding to each other with low levels of hope, but Martineau looked flushed and sour. He whispered in his lawyer's ear, and then turned to tug at Bergen's sleeve.

"Let's turn off their valves," someone yelled.

A gleeful yelp came from the back row. "Enough talk! We'll cement up their pipe lines."

"Mr. Martineau has asked for a chance at rebuttal," Bergen shouted, whacking the gavel on the desk with strong strokes, as if he were pounding a nail. "I know it's late, but we'll give him ten minutes for a wrap-up, and then we'll adjourn." He glared a threat across the room. "Ladies and gentlemen, give Mr. Martineau your attention, if you please."

The crowd quieted enough to hear, but the undertone of comments and whispers continued. Martineau got to his feet, walked to the front of the table and took the microphone, ignoring the guffaws and catcalls being flung at him. Twenty years before, he had been a rookie on the pro-golfing tour, his brief claim to fame. Now he was all corporate executive, his blossoming paunch disguised by the careful draping of an azure sports jacket, the Sonoran Skyline logo on the breast pocket. He turned to face the citizens of Chuparrosa, caressed his flowered tie, collected his fair, mottled face into a benign smile, and ran a hand over his thinning blond hair.

"Hey," he called to them, his warm baritone rippling through the speakers. "I live here, too. My family and I intend to stay in Chuparrosa. My wife has joined the Women's Club, my son's in Tempe at the University, and we have a friendly little pet named Curly. We, at Sonoran Skyline, consider the lovely town of Chuparrosa one of our finest amenities. We don't want any part of the town to run out of water." Roger's pale eyebrows curved wistfully above the center of his nose. "We at Sonoran Skyline and our parent company, Greenwood Development, your neighbor in Phoenix, want Chuparrosa to prosper and grow, just as you do."

There were growlings in the audience. Someone whooped, "What a bunch of shit!" Martineau cleared his throat and lumbered on.

"Chuparrosa's prosperity depends on her businesses. We don't want factories belching smoke and noise. We want serenity and beauty. That's what places like Sonoran Skyline will bring you – money from taxes and increased sales in your stores, both produced by a large population of contented homeowners like yourselves, working together to preserve the Sonoran lifestyle. This'll take time, but it will come. Golf courses are the magnets which attract new residents."

"There's not enough water in that aquifer for all those people and all that grass," roared Wendel Quinn from the second row. He punched the air above the top of his baldhead with bunched fists.

Roger attempted an agreeable laugh and pulled a handkerchief from a back pocket to mop his forehead. "Each of our golf courses occupy only 90 acres of land, instead of the usual 130 acres. Our technicians constantly monitor the computerized watering system to conserve water. As soon as we have enough homes in the development, we'll switch to effluent. The treatment plant is already in place. It'll be operational when two hundred homes are built. By the time we have a population of twenty five hundred, only reclaimed water will be used for irrigation."

"And how many years will that take while you pump away our non-renewable resource?" snarled Sugar Morley, under his nose in the front row. Other voices shouted their support.

"Our projection is that we can accomplish this goal in just five years," Roger shrilled, his smile wilting. "This is very desirable property. The courses are designed by pro-golfer, Wade Hawken, who has succeeded in creating exciting challenges for golfers of any expertise. Our second clubhouse is now being built of native stone, so as to blend into the desert environment. The xeriscape plantings will use almost no water and provide a lush habitat for birds and animals. Even now we have deer grazing on the fairways." He raised his eyes to the ceiling, awe spreading across his face at the anticipation of such beauty. "And we intend to place markers by each plant for identification."

"The deer will love that! Window dressing!" Sugar sprang to her feet. "I have to have water trucked in for my suffering horses, while you slop through grass so green it hurts my eyes." She launched herself forward, small fists clenched, gray curls bobbing, her face level with Martineau's Adam's apple, and began pounding his chest, destroying the symmetry of his tie.

Sanchez stepped behind her before she could do much damage, arms around her shoulders, hands sliding down to pull her fists away from the startled man. Out of the corner of his eye, he saw Kevin Dingle plant himself between the crowd and the table of guns. Good boy, Kevin.

"Come on, Mrs. Morley," Hank crooned in her ear. "Your don't need to do this. It's not going to help your horses any."

She flung him off with a look of loathing and turned to reach for the protective arms of her husband and sons.

"We can manage Momma ourselves." The older one, Jeremiah, spit the words out between his teeth, his voice dangerous, eyes slits of red.

Roger, the good-natured smile now a frozen grimace, backed up, still gripping the mike, to confer with his lawyer behind the shelter of the table.

"This meeting's adjourned!" Mel Bergen's voice boomed with finality from the public address system. "Turn out the lights back there, Deputy Dingle. We're going all home."

Chapter 2

Even with the lights dimmed, the crowd did not leave quickly. They clumped together in small groups, repeating their arguments in loud voices and shooting dirty looks over their shoulders at Mayor Mel Bergen and Roger Martineau. Reporter Tubbs, clutching her pad and pencil, circulated among them, furiously scribbling their quotes.

Sanchez loitered near the head table. A glance toward the exit assured him that Kevin was acting as a doorstop, joshing with the gun-owners as they picked up their side arms. One by one the citizens passed out to the plaza, heads bowed to face the wind, and eyes closed in the flying dust. The pungent smell of distant rain seeped into the room, but no drops of welcome water had fallen in Chuparrosa.

Martineau and his lawyer shoveled papers into their briefcases. With obvious relief, they hurried out through the heavy back door that Sanchez held open for them, nodding their thanks as they scuttled off into the stormy black night.

When the room cleared, Hank caught Dingle's eye and gave him the high sign to take off. They'd discuss the report of the night's activities in the morning. With a salute, the deputy vanished in the darkness of the plaza.

"I can't understand what they're so mad about." Mel shook his head and ran a hand through his graying hair. "That is one classy development. It's bound to attract the best people. They manicure each blade of grass on those courses. Did you know their first course got a four star rating from *Golfer's Globe* the year it was finished?"

Sanchez stared at his boots and wondered how much of a reality check Bergen could grasp. Since coming to Chuparrosa from his job as a detective with the Albuquerque police force, he'd learned to identify the serious golfers in the community. They were the ones who played every day of the year, even when the grandchildren came to visit. They went to Vegas only when a new course opened there. In their heads, the game blocked out all other points of view. He suspected Mel Bergen had one of those heads.

Some Chuparrosa winter residents were plunking down big bucks for lots in Sonoran Skyline, so they could play the three exclusive courses. It was considered a great investment, as well. Hank wasn't a golfer himself, and the devotion some golfers felt for the game puzzled him.

Now the town's permanent residents seemed to be pitted against the new development. These folks had been westerners most of their lives, used to a small town and big on homeowners' rights. Every fall, since their village had been "discovered" some eighteen years ago, visitors from the northern states had come to bask in the sunshine ten miles north of the hustle and bustle of Phoenix. The seasonal prosperity pleased the residents as long as the changes didn't come too fast. Sanchez suspected it was beginning to dawn on them that Greenwood Development could swallow them up. A corporate takeover of Chuparrosa. The water shortage, some felt, might be the hammer to beat off these money-grubbing meddlers and snatch back their town.

The mayor began clipping his papers together, selecting places for them in the pockets of his briefcase. "Well, at least that's over, and we got through it with no bloodshed." The humorless chuckle indicated he'd made a joke. He snapped the briefcase shut with the air of someone starting out on a holiday.

"Good job tonight, Hank. Kevin, too." He clapped his marshal on the shoulder. "Now all those people have had their say, the air has been cleared, and we'll hear no more about it. There's nothing the town can do about the golf course watering, after all. The wells on Sonoran Skyline are grandfathered with the county, so it's out of our hands." He frowned, considering. "We could, I guess, offer our citizens some classes in water management. What do you think?"

15

"According to Bud Brickson, the Citizens' Water Committee is meeting tomorrow night to map strategy, Mel," Sanchez said. "They're unhappy about the lack of water, and they expect the town to do something about it. Five hundred acres of Sonoran Skyline are in Chuparrosa city limits. We have to be responsible for maintaining the peace on that, like it or not. There are a few scrappy people on Spanish Saddle Mountain who live for confrontations, and they have a legitimate beef. The serious danger of losing their water supply will affect the value of their homes."

"Confrontations are okay." Mel gave his horn-rimmed glasses a boost up his nose and hefted the briefcase off the table. "We'll schedule another one any time they get the urge to yell at us. They're all law-abiding citizens, and they have to share the water in the aquifer, so that's pretty much the end of it. We've had a little drought, but it will rain again, and when it does things'll settle down. Next week I'll appoint a committee to begin work on a long range water plan for them, but for now they'll have to haul it in."

He turned on his heel and nearly collided with a portly gentleman wearing a rumpled madras sport shirt that curved down his belly and hung out over his chino trousers. A shock of unruly white hair added two inches to his diminutive height. Beaming, he extended his hand first to the mayor and then to the marshal.

"Milford Wheat's my name," he said, wheezing just a bit. "Excuse the cough. Emphysema. It's the dust that's bothering me tonight. I'm a whale of a lot better since I moved here from Florida." He smiled, his face folding into ruddy grooves around a mouthful of small, even teeth. His eyes, an odd golden color, shone with good humor. "I came here to dry out, you know. The humidity in Miami nearly killed me."

"Been here long, Mr. Wheat?" Bergen's voice indicated that he was rising to the occasion with some effort.

"Please call me Ford. Three weeks exactly. We bought a home in Chuparrosa for now, but I've also purchased a lot in Sonoran Skyline. Five rugged acres. It's in the county portion of the development, but we'll be in the town before long. As soon as there're enough residents to override the developer."

Sanchez noticed the interest growing on the mayor's face. Anyone with the millions necessary to buy five acres in the Skyline, and a desire to be a resident of Chuparrosa, was destined to be Mel's best friend.

"Moved here with your family, Ford?"

"Just my grandson. He has asthma, so we are both afflicted. This climate is better for him, as well. His mother likes to travel. Not the sort of life for a kid. I keep him with me and hire a housekeeper." He chuckled, and the golden eyes squeezed shut among the wrinkles that circled his face. "And we guys make out just fine."

Sanchez considered a preliminary estimate of Mr. Wheat: Santa Claus without a beard, a retired industrialist who golfs and votes Republican.

"Play golf, Ford?" Mel asked, getting down to essentials.

"Oh, you bet. That's why I bought in the Skyline. What great courses! Do you play there?"

The mayor gave an enthusiastic nod. "I bought a small lot in the Chuparrosa portion so I could use the courses. My duties with the town keep me busier than I like, but I get in three or four games a week. Call me at my office. I'll find a couple of other fellows for a foursome."

Sanchez began flipping off the remaining lights and PA system as the two men edged toward the plaza exit. Over the whine of the wind, he could hear the splatter of the first huge drops of rain. Good thing he'd rolled up the windows on his pickup.

The kicking began before they reached the door, a steady, urgent thud of feet, even louder than the roll of thunder. Yells, too, calling the marshal by name. Sanchez stepped in front of the mayor and cracked the door, bracing himself against the force of the wind.

Roger Martineau stood blinking on the threshold, mouth hanging loose. His blond hair stuck up in fragile points, like twigs, on top of his head. The blue jacket and flowered tie were missing. He wore no shoes. His water-soaked shirt and trousers clung to his lumpy body like a wrinkled skin, transparent over the rolls of fat on his chest.

The three men stared into Roger's shocked blue eyes and then down at the furry creature that lay unmoving in his arms.

"They killed him, a defenseless little dog," he coughed out in a whisper. His chin quivered and spasms shook his shoulders over and over in an involuntary rhythm. "In the pool. Those sonofabitches drowned him in my pool."

Chapter 3

By the time Sanchez had locked up the city council chamber and clambered into his pickup truck, the town clock was chiming a quarter of twelve. The monsoon had squeezed itself out to a few fitful drops. He switched on the wipers to sweep away the rain that dotted the glass and slumped over the steering wheel, feeling the clamminess of his uniform shirt across his shoulders, the weariness of the evening. Something inside him had revolted at the sight of that small dead dog, its shaggy head nestled on Martineau's arm. Hank thought of dogs he had owned, friendly animals, each one unique and full of life. The image of someone deliberately killing a pet made him scowl. If Roger was right, the killer could be a resident angered by tonight's meeting.

Hank shifted into gear and kept his foot on the break. Go home, he told himself, thinking how talking to Pella would smooth the rocky evening into a gentler landscape. She had a way of distilling his thoughts and then feeding them back to him with objectivity. No one else he'd found in this town of Anglos, rich, poor or middle class, was willing to be so straight with a Hispanic.

For the past six months, almost since the day they met, he'd been in love with her. So far he'd had to settle for a dissatisfying hands-off sort of romance. A lonely, uprooted childhood, the sudden death of her husband two years before and the April murder of her friend and employer in Chuparrosa had made her wary of any commitment. There'd been too many disturbing moments when she'd drawn away, her somber widowhood drifting between them like a cold mist. He'd been patient, but now his patience was as fragile as the ragged clouds he could see breaking up in the west. He didn't know how to beg a woman; he'd never had to. Coax, maybe, but never beg.

"Only when I'm whole," she'd told him the first time he'd pressed her to stay the night. "When I've had a chance to be myself for awhile, not someone's appendage." She looked him over with those candid gray eyes. "Maybe you won't like the person I turn out to be when I'm not grasping at a husband or a friend."

He doubted it, but since then, he'd given her the space she wanted. Space he was sure could be occupied more enjoyably by the two of them. She was lucky he was thirty-six. He'd been a headstrong kid at twenty, when he'd married Luisa, whose chief talent was passion. She'd been as wrong for him as he'd been for her. Maybe living on the fringes of the Anglo world for most of his adult life had erased the machismo of his *castizo* upbringing in a northern New Mexican village. He told himself that waiting heightened the excitement. But, damn it, enough was enough.

Hank broke into a laugh and, feeling plenty excited, spun his pickup into a u-turn, heading for Pella's apartment at the edge of town. He wondered how she'd react if he kicked in her door.

The pickup's tires sprayed water from the shallow puddles left by the rain of an hour ago. The smell of creosote bushes blew across his face through the open window. Not much moisture, he guessed, a few minutes of downpour, scrubbing dusty plants, plus a noisy display of lightning that hissed to Earth in brilliant electric streaks. The system had moved north and was probably refreshing Crown King or Bumble Bee by now. Winds died as the rain swept through. A black, silent peace had taken its place, broken only by the murmurings of the far-distant storm, like a hysterical child still sobbing in its sleep.

Early in the summer, Pella had changed apartments. Jobless and traumatized after her employer at the Cuthbert Gallery had been murdered, she'd done what she could to find her bearings and trim expenses. With her friend Glory Windom, she'd leased a cheaper, ground floor efficiency without tennis courts or pool. They'd merged their furniture and rented the rest. Since Glory worked days at the T-shirt Factory and nights at the Cactus Blossom Café in order to support a serious jewelry habit, she and Pella seldom saw one another. Their refrigerator, papered with notes, kept them in touch with each other's schedules and lives.

Hank swung his pickup into her driveway and loped to the door. It was wide open and welcoming. He grinned, shrugged his shoulders and re-caged the beast that had longed to beat it down.

Pella sat cross-legged on the floor, surrounded by piles of paper, her bare legs and bare feet were curled around an expandable file. Head bent, she studied a sheet of handwritten notes, her tousled blond hair drooping into her eyes. She looked up as he stepped in, surprise lighting her smile. Hank crouched on one knee, kissed her, and ran his hand down her face and throat to squeeze her shoulder. It was an intimate gesture that made her close her eyes with pleasure and sharpened his longing to the point of pain.

"This is nice. I'd given you up. It must have been an awful meeting." She put a hand on his arm to guide him as he rose. "Careful, now. Your boots are shuffling the precious remnants of my entire mind."

"Festival committee?" He stood and picked his way through the islands of paper toward the kitchen, where he rummaged in the refrigerator for two bottles of beer.

"I've finally persuaded the committee chairmen to turn over all their little decisions, so I can see the big picture and eliminate surprises. At first they thought it was so strange that the festival producer should get caught up in their plans. Now they're at me every minute. I've got to get this mess organized before a wind blows it all the way to Tucson."

She stared at the piles of paper circling her, everything from whole sheets and sticky notes to a matchbook cover or two. "This is the last of the paper trail. I'm going to try to decipher 'em tomorrow and enter 'em into the computer. In the meantime, they'll be at my toe tips." She squinted at a phone number jotted onto a corner torn from a newspaper and pulled a pencil from behind her ear to darken the numbers. "Unless I decide to just touch a match to the whole collection and watch them go up in flames." She grinned. "We could roast marshmallows. No?

Well then, final countdown. Ten days till F-day. And don't raise your eyebrows. That's F for Festival."

The mayor thinks you're a genius," said Hank. He laced his fingers around the necks of two bottles and searched in a drawer for an opener. "Nobody can figure out how you pulled that gang of goof-offs together."

In July, when the plans for a festival to mark 125th anniversary of the founding of Chuparrosa began to flounder under the leadership of the mayor's wife, Sanchez, mindful of Pella's shaky finances, had persuaded the mayor to hire her as part time Festival coordinator. Then a month ago she'd taken a second job as part time receptionist/secretary to Roger Martineau. Between her mornings at Sonoran Skyline Development and afternoons in a tiny office in the city hall complex, she was grubbing her way to solvency.

"You're the wise guy who got me this job. At the time I wasn't very grateful." Pella reached up for the bottle of beer Hank handed her.

"How grateful are you now?"

She tipped back her golden head to take a sip, and sighting off the end of the bottle, gave him a long, undefined look before dropping her eyes. "How did the water meeting go?" she asked. "Was everybody horrid?"

"Well, lively anyway. It was quite a pow-wow. I thought for a while we wouldn't get out of there without an uprising. Sugar Morley tried to beat up on Roger Martineau, but I managed to pull her off." Sanchez sank into one of the armchairs, upholstered in blue denim, and stretched his long legs out carefully on either side of Pella's papers.

"Sugar!" Her gray eyes were scornful. "She couldn't have done much damage. Did you hurt her?"

"Not with her men-folk standing by. She's a scrappy lady. She knew Roger wouldn't dare defend himself. He was scared to death of her bodyguards. Wise man. So was I." He grinned at her, rubbing his knuckles over the gritty stubble of late-day beard, knowing he should go to his own place, but relaxing now, enjoying the company. And the view.

"So the people on wells are not going to be satisfied by one town meeting?"

"Not by a long shot. It didn't settle anything. Half a century ago the water rights on Sonoran Skyline's land were for ranchers and their cattle. Stock tanks, ponds and the family garden. Nobody could have predicted that Martineau would use the aquifer to grow grass all over a desert valley, where grass has never grown before, so a few hundred privileged people could play a game. Maybe Roger could gain some points by offering a free membership for every dry well."

"Not a golfer in the bunch, though, except for Bud Brickson. They're all horse and dog people." Pella spun around on her bottom and danced onto her toes to step beyond the mess of papers. Slipping onto the other denim chair, she knelt on the cushion and leaned toward him over the arm. "What will you do now?"

Hank, admiring her as she moved, had been wondering, uselessly, whether she had anything on under the tank top and shorts. "Mm-mm. The mayor believes it's all been taken care of, so he's ready to talk to the council about a long-range solution. Or he was until Roger turned up again with his dog."

"Roger brought his dog? Curly? That little Benji animal? That's not at all like our Roger in business mode."

Sanchez leaned back against the high cushion, frowning, remembering. "The dog was dead, Pella. Drowned." He thought back to the sight of Martineau's trembling anger and the sodden bundle he had clutched to his chest as he stood in the doorway, wind-whipped by the storm. It had taken a slow, trying hour to convince him that the marshal would do everything to catch the culprit, but nothing could be done in the dark. It would have to wait till morning. The man was still shaking when he left city hall.

"When Roger got home from the meeting, he searched the patio where they'd left Curly and found him at the bottom of the pool." Hank turned his scowl in Pella's direction. "Roger said the dog was used to swimming in the pool with his wife and could get in and out by himself on the steps. He believes someone caught Curly and held him under until he stopped squirming."

"How ghastly!" Pella's troubled eyes searched his face. "Was Mrs. Martineau home?"

"No one was home. She'd gone to Scottsdale to play bridge with friends, and the dog had been left on the enclosed patio. He couldn't get out. The gate was locked. It wouldn't have been too hard to get into the patio by stepping on the enclosure around the pool equipment and climbing over the wall. They'd set the inside alarm system, but not the motion detector on the patio, because Curly was out there. After all, it's a gated community. People rely on that."

Sanchez drank the last of his beer and set the bottle on the tiled floor. He had no desire to leave, but longed to take off his boots and the tan uniform he'd worn since six that morning. "I'll stop over at Martineau's tomorrow and have a look around." He tried to smother a yawn and failed.

"Poor Roger! He adored that little dog, always bragging about the tricks he'd taught him." Pella rested her chin on one hand. "This whole thing is pretty sick. What's the motive?"

"Roger's convinced it's the first strike by folks on Spanish Saddle Mountain. He'd just been battered by Sugar Morley. Those two boys of hers look like young thugs. Most of the Mountain people are crazy about animals, at least their own. If it turns out to have been an execution, we might find some sort of message."

Hank rubbed the space between his eyes. The first sight of Roger's small dead pet had captured all his attention. The feelings of apprehension were hard to shake. He had trouble believing that someone in Chuparrosa could have committed such a savage act.

"What if a coyote jumped the wall and chased Curly into the pool?" Pella asked. "He might have treaded water as long as he could, while the coyote circled, and then slipped under."

"A coyote would've caught him and treated his friends to a feast. An owl would have taken him off, too. When Nature provides a meal, it's consumed. The killer wanted Roger to find a body."

Pella twisted her fingers together around the neck of the brown bottle. "You're truly worried about this," she said. "How did

Greenwood Development get all that lovely land on the creek, anyway?"

"They did a land and cash swap about ten years ago. Thirty six hundred acres of BLM land here in the heart of things for a lot of cash and an even larger piece of undeveloped land they owned northwest of the Grand Canyon. Five hundred acres lies in the Chuparrosa city limits and the rest in the county. People say it was a shrewd deal even for Arizona. As usual, nobody thought about the impact until they realized the wells were going dry. At the moment, it's just the wells up on Spanish Saddle. But not everyone lower down in Chuparrosa is hooked up to the city system either, so there's a potential for more problems."

Hank leaned forward, elbows on his knees. "Now there's too much anger and too little water. As long as Sonoran Skyline sucks up the aquifer for their golf courses, the people on the Mountain will be dry and drier. If the development stops watering, their grass will die and their sales with it. From what you tell me business isn't exactly booming."

"Maybe a bit sluggish. There are fifty or sixty houses now and two courses, with a third in the planning. Many lots have been sold." Her face was thoughtful. "So who's to blame? We have two groups of decent people with different needs and different points of view."

"And my job is to keep them from killing each other." Sanchez pulled himself out of the blue chair and planted his boots between the papers littering the rug.

"You're not seriously suggesting a civil war?"

"I didn't think so at first, but this is the West, *querida,* where liquor is for drinking and water is for fighting. *Agua es la vida.* In the desert, it's also power and has been since prehistoric times. At the scent of water the greedy start to circle. There's never enough of it, and it's always in the wrong place."

He forced a big smile, giving her an appreciative once-over. "I'm going to leave you. Walk me out to the pickup, *cara mia,* and give me a big send off."

Her bare legs uncoiled, and she came out of her chair with a laugh. "You get so courtly at this time of night." she said. "I've noticed it before."

"Someday you'll be unable to resist my *Hidalgo* charm." Hank opened the screen door with a flourish, and they stepped out into the filmy warmth of the humid night. Desert scents reached them as the rain-dampened plants filled the air with their perfume. She took his arm, stepping across the bricks in her bare feet. When they got to the pickup, away from the front light, she stretched up to kiss him.

"Thanks for coming over, Hank." She smoothed her fingers across the worry lines between his eyes. "Sleep well."

It had been easier, he reflected, when he didn't have anyone to say these things to him. Maybe Pella had it right when it came to leaning on someone else. A little sympathy and understanding made him want more. Especially when it was so neatly packaged. He pulled the package closer, burying his face in her hair, then kissing her again, with more urgency.

She eased herself out of his arms. "Time for you to go home, *amigo mio.*"

Hank let her go, but cupped her face between his hands. "If I were your lover, I could still be your friend," he explained, expecting no reply. "Be careful the next few weeks, Pella. You work for the two employers most likely to be targets if tempers get out of control. Whoever would kill a dog for just for spite must have a lot at stake. Let me know immediately if anything strange happens at work. And don't accept any odd invitations."

Pella heard the roar of the pickup motor as she trotted back to her door. She passed through the living room, snatching up the empty beer bottles to stow them in the recycling bin. The light blinked on her answering machine. Had it rung while she stood outside with Hank? It was past midnight. Probably someone on the Festival Committee. Those people thought they owned her. Jeez!

Annoyed, she pushed the play button and heard a man's voice, a sensual purr with an overriding snarl, heavy with menace.

"Bitch," the voice swore, "tell your lover boy we got the dog. If Martineau doesn't turn off the valves to those goddamn courses by Friday noon you'll take the next swim."

Chapter 4

Agatha Pure Stone stepped with care along the bank of Devil's Eye Creek, through a brittle tangle of cat claw and grasses that crunched like potato chips beneath her soft leather boots. The fringes fluttering at the bottom of her muslin dress snagged the chaff, collecting buffle grass like a trim of scraggly fur. At each step the woven sash, securing the garment to the dumpling of her waist, swung out before her, slashing at the path.

Her gray hair, parted from forehead to nape, hung in two braids down her back. A beaded leather band encircled her head. That morning Agatha had painted her face, tanned and grooved by years of exposure to the Sun. The design, a jagged lightning symbol, glowed on each cheek. She walked briskly, with a sinewy sense of anticipation. She was almost there, in the presence of the Mystery.

Nothing marred the perfect iridescence of the dawn sky. In the hush of first light, only the birds moved, chirping and darting about in their constant search for food.

In the Creek, five round, white stones, their tops smoothed by centuries of floods, bulged above the sluggishly lapping water. Their spacing demanded a daring leap into the stream, three balanced placements of the feet, and a swinging step to catch the mesquite tree that clung with naked roots to the opposite bank.

Without a pause, Agatha hiked up her skirt, stepped with agility from stone to stone, leaped onto the lower rungs of the roots and scrambled to more stable footing above. Bending low, she plunged into the mesquite bosque on the other side, scarcely feeling the branches clawing at her clothes and raising welts on her bare arms. Beyond the bosque was a park-like space covered with stone outcroppings and here and there a hop bush. Agatha paused as she reached it, her face wrinkling into a deep smile that pleated the lightning symbols on her cheeks.

Up in the clear, wide sky a jet droned, and somewhere far away a dog barked. There was no other sound, until a thrasher on top of a saguaro lifted its head to herald the hot edge of sun showing over the eastern mountains

Agatha raised her arms at right angles to her body, hands parallel to her head and began a hesitation step, shifting from one foot to the other in time to a chant. Her slow progression took her towards a circle of stones seventy feet across. At the circle's edge, she fell to her knees, and with arms high above her head, eyes shut, she went on with her chant.

Agatha Pure Stone had been a Native American for twenty of her sixty years. Before that, in what she referred to as a former life, she was Sally Pastorelli, a secretary in Baltimore. Around the age of forty, she'd felt flutterings of discontent, and while on a bus tour of Arizona came to understand that this would mean a change of identity. She moved to Phoenix, where she spent her days at the library and the Heard Museum studying the lore of the Hohokam, the prehistoric people who had vanished from the Salt River lands long before any Europeans straggled there across the desert. A year later she quietly evolved into a Hohokam medicine woman.

Metamorphosis complete, Agatha bought an acreage on the fringe of Devil's Eye Creek, where she puddled adobe mud over streambed stones to make herself a hut, and began giving lectures on her spirit life with the Hohokam. Her programs included interpretive dances, chants, fortune telling and exhortations on preserving the Sonoran Desert. She had honed her skills and patter to such a degree that some innocents thought her to be all she said. There was no doubt that she believed it herself.

Agatha often drifted through Chuparrosa's stores in her homemade garb, offering advice and Hohokam homilies to anyone who had a moment for her. She was in much demand for house blessings. The fees she charged paid her taxes and incidentals. Residents might laugh at her, but they respected her childlike sincerity. Tourists adored her, and whatever the tourists liked, Chuparrosans liked, too. She had become as much a part of the town's ambience as the fancy shops that scalloped Gold Dust Road and the mock gun battles Charlie Taleferro held outside his Miner's Delight Saloon.

Agatha Pure Stone completed her chant and gave a last wail, before she got stiffly to her feet and moved into the circle to face the first stone. On its black, desert-varnished side was a petroglyph, a design of goat-like animals. They pranced from top to bottom, some upright, others topsy-turvy, all thick bodied, four legged, with horns curving to wicked points.

She had stumbled across the old stones her first year in Arizona, and realizing it was an ancient shrine, had bought land close to it. She had been told that the land where the shrine sat belonged to the Bureau of Land Management and was being held by the U.S. Government as a potential trade or consolidation parcel. Since it wasn't for sale in small lots, she had contented herself with being a neighbor. At the time of each full moon, she crept down Devil's Eye Creek to commune with her ancestral spirits.

The September Sun rose over the mesquite and willow bordering the creek until it shone hotly down on Agatha Pure Stone, making drops of sweat glisten above the beaded band. She circled the stones, saluting each form of animal life in turn – lizards, quail, deer, coyotes, bobcats, spiders, snakes and man. Birdsong pierced the silence. A breeze sprang up, shivering the grasses. She'd almost completed the circle, her face aglow with pleasure from her ardent meditations, when she became aware to her horror that the headstone was missing.

Her mouth gaped open in astonishment as she stared at the empty space, at the hole where the rock had rested for a thousand years. It was the signature stone of the group, the most sacred. On it were the life signs that protected all the petroglyphic creatures, its swirls depicting the life cycles of abundance from Earth. She held this stone in the greatest reverence. Life linked all creatures together.

Agatha dropped to the ground and sat cross-legged, her eyes fixed on the empty hole. The grasses had been trampled around the depression, and she could see a fresh trail of bent undergrowth heading off toward the bluff edging the wider creek bed. Any footprints had been washed away by the shower of the night before. The headstone was larger than the rest. It would have needed two people, with a lever and wheels, to pry it out and cart it off.

She knew people sometimes came here. In the past she'd had to pick up pop cans and candy wrappers, but there were stiff penalties for removing artifacts. She shuddered in shocked disbelief. Who would dare defile a sacred set?

While the Sun kept climbing, Agatha stayed motionless, thinking. The muslin dress grew wet with sweat, and gnats, attracted by the moisture, sang about her head, diving to settle on damp places. She flicked at them with her braids.

Near noon she rose unsteadily, cramps paining her aging knees as they straightened out once more. She aimed a shrewd glance at the sky. Clouds were building on the eastern horizon. Perhaps it would shower again so she'd have enough water to bathe. If it didn't, Devil's Eye Creek would have to do. No plumbing at Agatha's hut.

She shook such impious thoughts aside. Returning the life stone to its place in the circle was of first importance. All other plans must be postponed until she'd restored the sanctity of the shrine. She turned back to the Creek, reluctant to abandon the remaining petrogylphs, and with dragging steps began the three-mile hike into Chuparrosa to see Ranger Bent at the National Forest Office. They weren't the best of friends. She knew he thought her strange, but in the desert they shared common interests, common goals. She'd beg him to help her find the stone.

Agatha Pure Stone pulled the muslin sleeve across her forehead, sponging up the drops of sweat, as she pushed her way back through the mesquite trees along the Creek. The damp dress hugged her body, and blue paint from the lightning zigzags streaked down her face.

"They will die," she said in a whisper of despair. "Without the life sign all animals will die."

Tyler Bent, archaeologist for the National Forest Service, tried not to look at the disheveled woman standing before his desk, her spooky eyes filled with both despair and hope. He picked up the telephone and punched in the marshal's number.

"They'll all die out there without the life stone, the animals, the humans, everything. In Nature we're all one," she repeated again.

He heard the ring and then the dispatcher's voice. "Linda? Tyler Bent, here. Give me the marshal, would you?"

Hank probably wouldn't know anything about the bloody rock, either, but Bent hoped that if he made some sort of effort, Agatha'd go back to her adobe hut and leave him be.

"Say, Hank, you know that little piece of BLM land by Devil's Eye Creek? It was the second trade to Greenwood Development for Sonoran Skyline. Just a few months ago. Yeah, BLM got more land near the Canyon for it." He rattled on as he saw Agatha's growing agitation. "Well, there's a ring of standing petroglyphs on the property. They had a survey done when it was traded."

Bent figured he'd seen them. Hank had ridden and hiked all over the area. But the man had this water thing on his mind now. Not a good time to bother him about missing rocks.

"Sure, you know the place. Well, Agatha Pure Stone is here reporting that the headstone is gone."

He hunched his shoulders, clad in the dull green Forest Service shirt, and holding the phone close to his ear, heard a groan. Agatha was on a different planet most of the time and could bother the hell out of you. Like those gnats that were so bad this month.

"She came to see if I knew where it was. I told her I'd check with you." He cupped his hand around the receiver and his mouth, as the woman turned away to glance out the window. "She keeps saying the animals will die without the headstone," he hissed. "I know it's their land now, and they can do whatever they want with it, but I thought maybe one of your guys had seen that stone in somebody's yard."

Agatha's head swiveled back to center, as hope flared in her eyes.

"Haven't seen it, huh? You'll have your patrol to keep watch for it? Yeah, I'll ask her, so we'll be prepared." This last in a whispered tone. "Thanks."

Bent looked up at his guest. "Sorry, Agatha, the marshal hasn't seen it, but he'll ask his patrols to check and alert Sonoran Skyline. Now don't get desperate," he added, as her whole body appeared to shrivel at the news. He couldn't have the woman blubbering in his office. "It's their land, legal and up front. They wanted to add that piece to Sonoran Skyline. It was traded to them three months ago for some more land near the Canyon. Happens all the time. If you'd read the papers, you'd know that. Nothing secret about the deal, at all. Sonoran Skyline wanted a creek-side piece for their fourth golf course. It's going to be a fancy place up there."

He leaned back in his chair, reading the thoughts behind her horrified expression. "Yeah, well, I'd rather have desert, too, but these guys have the big bucks. I guess they think they can sell a bunch of houses up here out of the smog."

"The animals will die." Agatha's voice throbbed with urgency. "The wise ancestors placed those rocks there long ago as a sign of the gods' protection. Without the life sign they will die. I know they will."

To the glum Bent, it sounded like a broken record. He studied the sweep of papers on his desk. He had to get back to work, to clear this mess into the files and be free to check a tampered site this afternoon. He shared her distress. No archaeologist could bear having antiquities destroyed, but he'd been around Arizona long enough to know the rights of individuals on their own land. If BLM had wanted to save that circle of stones, they should've taken them when the survey was made. Agatha wouldn't have liked that, either.

He stood up, stepped around the desk, and placed his hand between her shoulder blades, pushing her toward the door. Head down, she offered no resistance.

"Look, Agatha, I'll do what I can." Bent gritted his teeth as he promised. "But we have no rights there. They could even have you arrested for trespassing. Come back next week, and I'll let you know what I've found out. The animals won't die that fast." He deposited her in the narrow hallway, filling the way back with his body and the half-closed door.

"By the way," Bent asked, as she shuffled off, "what will you do if we find the rock?"

Agatha Pure Stone glanced back over her shoulder. "Why, put it back where it belongs, of course," she said, staring at him as if he were the eccentric one. "We can't let the animals die."

Chapter 5

Marshal Sanchez hung up the phone and stared out of his office window at Gold Dust Road, Chuparrosa's glossy main street, as it simmered in the 96-degree heat of a late September afternoon. For most shoppers this was the hour of siesta. Only a man and a woman, both wearing shorts and tank tops, were strolling in the shade of a portico fronting six tiny boutiques, which sold everything from T-shirts to jewelry and art work. Searching for souvenirs for the folks back home he guessed. They looked miserable as they bent over ice cream cones, sweeping their tongues around surfaces that oozed sticky streams down to their hands.

The regular winter visitors were starting to come back to Chuparrosa. Like migrating birds, they'd retreated to more moderate climes during the blistering summer. As Arizona nights cooled and days grew shorter, the town's population doubled. Then the lives of the permanent residents, shopkeepers, city staffers, realtors, small ranchers and service people, burst into activity.

Each new arrival added to the duties of the marshal and his staff. With the conflict over water threatening to divide the town into warring camps, Sanchez knew he couldn't spare much time searching for Agatha's petroglyph.

Swiping petroglyphs from private or public land was common in unpopulated areas. Not much anyone could do about it, either. Residents came back from vacation to find the chipped rock art, that had lain undisturbed for centuries, had been carted away from their front yards. Or the thieves split off the picture portion, leaving half the rock staring out at the desert with a fresh, blank face. The dark stones were valuable trophies for dealers or collectors. Nearly untraceable and unredeemable, they vanished with no one the wiser, and their ancient incised designs soon graced a new home.

Sanchez tossed his pen onto the desk and scribbled his fingers through his hair. He had a low opinion of people who walked off with Arizona's past. Pot hunters. Petroglyph swipers. *¡Pinche hombres!* If it were up to him, he'd load the whole bloody shrine into his pickup, take it to Agatha's place and let her look after it. But, damn it, they belonged to Sonoran Skyline, and if the life stone turned up, he'd have to give it back to them.

Not that the gesture would bring him any satisfaction. He doubted that developers who scraped off all the desert vegetation, that had evolved to succeed in this harsh environment, could be trusted with an ancient monument. The gaudy green of Sonoran Skyline's lush fairways mocked the desert vegetation's astonishing achievements at adaptation. Sanchez preferred to accept Nature on her own merits.

He reached for the phone and dialed Louise Ruskin's number. Maybe the local archaeology club would be interested. The stone shrine was well known. They would have mourned its loss to the development. When she answered, he described the vandalism in a few words.

"But that's shocking, Hank," she sputtered. "Some people have no reverence for the past. I'll drive out to see Agatha, and then the club will organize some search parties."

"You realize it could be out of state by now."

She sighed. "I know, but if it's here we'll track it down. Some of our members aren't back yet, but I have about twenty dedicated stewards I can rally. If we find it, we'll hold it for ransom until Roger Martineau promises to protect them all." She gave a brisk laugh. "Now don't rat on us, Marshal."

He hung up the phone, retrieved his pen and got back to the notes he'd made on the death of Martineau's dog. Roger had left for his office by the time Hank arrived at his home, eight thousand square feet of professionally over-decorated living space. It was modern Southwest, with enormous rooms, a two-story foyer, red tile roof and odd bay windows jutting in all directions. Leanne Martineau, shoulder-length brown hair held back with a headband that matched her blue checked jumpsuit, had handed him a cup of coffee and marched him out to the spacious walled patio, where a sweep hummed around the edges of a tiled pool. At one end, water bubbled from a fountain disguised as a natural rock formation. Coral bougainvillea blossoms bobbed in the sunshine.

"I went to Scottsdale for bridge with my old group last night," Leanne said, scowling at the sparkling water. "We still meet once a week in each other's homes. Eight of us. We've been playing together for twelve years, ever since Roger and I moved to the Valley. They're my oldest friends." She pulled off her dark glasses and brushed a hand across her eyes. "But hell, it cost the life of our dog."

"What time did you come back?"

"Eleven-thirty. By that time Roger had found Curly and was howling like a banshee." She choked on the last word and jammed the glasses back on her face. "Why, in God's name, would anyone want to hurt a little dog?"

"How do you know it wasn't an accident?"

Leanne strode to the far edge of the pool, her scarlet sandals clicking on the cool deck. Classy looking woman, Sanchez thought, as he followed her. Tall and tan, early forties, and still slim from year-round exercise.

"Do you play golf at Sonoran Skyline, Mrs. Martineau?"

Frowning, she turned to stare at him. "No way. Tennis is my game. This family doesn't need any more ardent golfers. Roger is enough."

She pointed into the depths of a bougainvillea vine that grew to the top of the five-foot wall and splayed out beyond it toward the desert. A piece of butcher's paper had been stuffed between its thorny branches. "Alfredo found that this morning when he came to do the pool. He was going to pitch it, but I realized what it contained, so I put it back. It looks about the way it did when he brought it to me. It's full of meat. Steak."

36

Sanchez pulled on gloves and scooped out the crumpled paper, touching it as little as possible. Inside was the steak, turning black in the sun. Ants crawled on the places where it had been gnawed by sharp teeth. The underside looked fresher. It couldn't have been exposed to the weather more than twelve hours.

"You're sure it wasn't here yesterday?"

"Curly was here yesterday," said Leanne. "He'd never pass up a treat like this." She swung back toward the shade and picked up her coffee mug with trembling fingers. "You know what bugs me? That monster didn't even let him eat the steak. He just caught the little guy and held him under."

"Anything else disturbed? How did he get into the patio?"

"He knocked St. Francis for a loop when he climbed over the wall. I told Alfredo to leave that mess, too."

She waved a hand at the pile of rubble Hank had dismissed as rocks. He crouched to inspect the broken pieces of Mexican pottery more closely. The head, a hand with the usual dove and the tapered body, split into four sections, lay on the granite chips near the cool deck. The pedestal, from which St. Francis had offered a blessing on the garden, rested on its side. Taking a look over the wall, Hank could understand how easy it would be for anyone over the age of ten to climb into the patio. The wall around the pool equipment formed irregular steps.

"The neighbors didn't hear any noise?"

"They're all several lots away. Roger can't ask them, in any case. The sales climate is always the bottom line with him." There was an ironic tone to her voice. "We can't afford to make anyone nervous."

"Curly wasn't a barker?" He'd known of neighbors who dispatched dogs that kept them awake at night.

"Usually no one gets close enough to the house to worry him. And he loved everybody except the man who reads the gas meter."

"It seems someone went for a stroll in your gated community on a stormy night armed with a piece of meat. I'll check with the gate attendant, but this person could have slipped in on foot from almost any point." He dropped the paper of meat into a plastic bag and jotted notes on the label. "This'll go in the freezer. Deputy Dingle will be over to take fingerprints this afternoon." Kevin could use the practice. Fingerprints were not usually definitive, and between the rain and Alfredo, Sanchez didn't have much hope. The meat paper held more possibilities. Maybe they could get some leads, at least. "Please keep everyone out of the patio until he's through."

Hank picked up his clipboard. "I'm sorry about Curly, Mrs. Martineau. Pella told me he was a great little dog."

"Oh, are you a friend of Pella's?" she asked, without enthusiasm. "Who could have done such a dreadful thing to that adorable dog?"

"Is there anything more I should know, ma'am?"

She shook her head and shuddered, "I may never swim in that pool again."

After Leanne showed him out, Sanchez had driven the curving block and a half to the Sonoran Skyline sales office to see what comments Roger had to offer. Pella had looked up from her computer with a big smile as he stepped through the massive doorway. Her sleeveless knit dress, the color of her gray eyes, had a scooped out neck and a clingy attitude. A necklace of glossy fake peppers filled in the scoop and little clusters of them swayed in her ears when she turned her head to smile a welcome.

"The boss is out playing golf with clients." She consulted her watch. "They've just teed off, so don't expect to catch up with him for five or six hours. It's a big day – an amateur invitational tournament we've been planning for so long. A shotgun, followed by a nineteenth hole and a fancy lunch. They're spread out all over three courses. Shall I put you on his 'call soon' list?"

"You won't be here when he gets back."

"No, but I leave wonderfully instructive memos when I go to lunch. And I have the power to put your name right at the top of the list." She scribbled on a pad and then looked up. "Curly's death was an accident, right?"

"No, it was deliberate. There was enough beefsteak around to bribe a pack of unfriendly Dobermans. A small, affectionate dog wouldn't have had a chance."

Her eyes widened, and she looked down at her keyboard, chewing her lip. Hank studied her a moment before he eased himself onto the corner of her desk.

"Tell me, Pella," he said. "Right now."

She tossed her head back making the blond hair fan out to the side and took a deep breath. "I thought it might be a joke. This message on my answering machine after you left last night. Something about getting the dog and then getting me if the water isn't turned off on the golf courses." Her gray eyes were serious, puzzled. "It doesn't make sense. Threatening Leanne might, but why me? I don't mean anything to Roger."

A clammy sensation prickled the back of Hank's neck. "Is the message still on your machine?"

"I erased it. No point in frightening Glory."

"A joke that was too frightening for Glory? Did you recognize the voice?"

She fingered the peppers on her necklace. "It was a man. I don't know anyone who sounds that slimy."

"Can you remember exactly what he said?" He could feel his face freezing into the expression Pella called his *bandido* look. "Repeat it for me," he demanded

She wiggled her shoulders. "I'll…write it." Her nails clicked on the keyboard. She changed a word or two and printed it.

"You should have called me about this last night." Hank studied the sheet she'd handed him. "The man knows where you live. He was right there on your street last night. He sat in his car, making the call, watching us outside. He saw me leave, and you were alone with the door wide open. Do I have your attention now?" He forced himself to sound calm.

"Well, maybe. But you would have come flying back to spend the night. You had enough on your mind. I was going to tell you today. From what he said, I'm safe and sound until Friday." Pella pushed back her chair, lifted a stack of files from her desk, and began hanging folders in an open drawer.

Hank stowed the paper in his shirt pocket, watching her, angry at her nonchalance. "Tomorrow's Friday! What will you do then?"

"Stay away from swimming pools, I guess. Good thing I moved out of that fancy apartment with all the amenities." She shot him a flushed, over-the-shoulder look.

Walking around the desk, he put his hands on her shoulders and swung her toward him. "This guy called from a cell phone outside your house, Pella. The blackmail is supposed to work on me. He knows I won't let anything happen to you. He figures I'll turn the water off myself, if I can't make Roger do it." He watched her eyes widen as he spoke. The important thing was to be frightened and smart, not frightened and hysterical. "You gonna be cool?"

She raised her chin and gave him a shaky smile. "You know what an Anglo-Saxon ice cube I am."

"Mm—yeah. Now get on the phone and find someone to bring Roger back here. He can't be much beyond the second hole. Send one of the grounds keepers to entertain the rest of the foursome."

"You know I can't do that. You'll have a murder on your hands."

"I can do it in the interest of public safety. You've been threatened by a stranger, and there's a whole new element mixed into the water."

"All right, but be prepared for an explosion," Pella warned. She picked up the phone and began to push buttons.

Hank strolled around the office, half his mind searching for ideas among the handsome displays hanging behind Plexiglas frames. There were layouts of the entire project, architectural drawings of the massive stone clubhouse now under construction and dreamy photographs of virgin golf courses at dawn, oases of rolling turf, like bumpy billiard tables, between lines of saguaros and ocotillos. Interspersed among the pictures, bright red and black Ganado rugs collided with the lush images of grass. The marketing was greedily upscale and exclusive. No answers for him there.

Was some sort of siege about to be forced on the town of Chuparrosa? Who, on the newly formed water committee, was mean enough to kill a pet and threaten Pella's life in order to get their way? He knew them all. None of the names fit that description.

"The marshal needs to talk to him right away, Ben," Pella said into the phone. Just roll over on a golf cart and find him. He can't be much farther than the second green. It's too important to explain over the phone." She paused, listening. "What's going on there, Ben? Ben!"

She put down the receiver, looking mystified. "Mass confusion at the golf lodge. Lots of shouting all of a sudden. Want to walk over and see what's happening?"

Hank flipped open the shutters on a nearby window that overlooked the third hole of Palo Verde Course. Towering sprays of water were swaying gracefully back and forth, rainbows reflected in the thick curtain of drops. A drenched foursome huddled off to one side, in the rough, regarding the sprinklers with hostility, as they tried to dry themselves with their golf towels.

"Is that part of the day's activities?"

Pella joined him at the window and began to laugh. "That's why I lost Ben. He's the day man on the grounds. Don't those guys look furious! All the pretty yellow trousers are soaked to a soggy mess." She clicked her tongue and giggled. "The sprinklers are on a timer, set to go on at dusk and run the required time. Somebody's goofed up the program. Or did last night's storm shut off the electricity?"

"Not for more than a couple of minutes. Where are the controls to set the timers?"

"It's all programmed by computer. There's a room in the maintenance building that contains the equipment. Each hole has to be set separately."

"How could it be changed? Could it be hacked into?"

"It wouldn't be too difficult to get into the room and re-program the schedule. Pick a couple locks and go to work. Nearly anyone who is computer literate could figure it out."

"Night watchman?"

"One night patrol and the guard at the gate. The patrol drives a random route, mostly in the areas where there are homes."

"How hard would it be to walk into the development?"

"Elementary, my dear Watson," Pella said. "It would be a breeze. I guess Curly's drowning proves that."

"That's the kind of prank some of the Spanish Saddle Mountain people might have dreamed up," Hank mused. "It may be against the law, but it doesn't hurt anyone. See, now they've turned it off."

There was a stamping at the door and Roger Martineau clattered in, his face the color of the peppers on Pella's necklace. His white knit shirt and brown checked plus fours, once natty, were soaked and splattered with mud. His golf shoes squished as he walked. Behind him, also red faced but smiling, bobbed the snowy head of Milford Wheat.

"Damn sprinklers went on!" Roger howled and swept one hand across his disheveled hair. "Just when we were on the second green. Bending down to putt and all of a sudden we're under a waterfall."

Drops collected in his hair and streamed down his angry face. Pella stepped into the powder room and came back with towels.

"Damn!" He panted, out of breath. "Make out Ben's check, Pella. He's leaving us!" Handing one of the towels to Wheat, Roger began mopping his face and arms. "Just when every hole on every course is full of guests!" He let out a string of oaths and swung his inflamed face toward Hank. "And what in bloody hell do you want that can't wait?"

"Pella," Hank said, "have you met Mr. Wheat?"

"Yes." She smiled. "We've been seeing a good deal of Mr. Wheat lately."

"'Ford,' my dear, remember?" The older man beamed. "Roger, I'm sure the marshal has vital information for you. Why don't I visit with Pella until you're free and then we'll catch up to the others. I might get a decent score if I get to skip a couple of holes."

"This concerns Pella, too," Hank said. "She received a threatening phone call last night." He handed the paper Pella had given him to Martineau, who dropped the towel onto an upholstered chair and settled himself on it. Wheat did the same, spreading the towel with care and perching on the edge of the chair, hands on his plump thighs.

Roger read the lines twice before he squinted up at Sanchez. "They are determined to persecute me, aren't they?" he growled. "First my dog, then the sprinklers and now they want to harm my staff. Well, Roger Martineau and Greenwood Development are not going to lie down for them. If they want a fight, by God, we'll circle the wagons and give it to 'em!"

Pella gave Hank a look somewhere between surprise and disbelief.

"¡Que va!" he thought, remembering Roger's quick retreat in the face of Sugar Morley's attack the night before. "If you only watered the greens for a few days, how long would the fairways last?"

"Thirty-six hours," Martineau snorted and lowered his head as if he might charge at the marshal. "You can forget any ideas of that kind, Sanchez. I refuse to even discuss 'em. We have every legal right to this water and a huge investment to protect, so nothing gets turned off."

"Then let's talk about a plan for the next few days while I do some investigating," Hank said. "You'll have to hire more night guards, one stationed in the maintenance building, one at the clubhouse construction site and one or two on foot among the houses. Warn the residents to expect them, so they don't start calling us about prowlers."

"What about Pella?" Ford Wheat asked. "I didn't see the note, but it seems to me that you need to give her some protection."

"I'll take care of those arrangements," Hank assured him. "We'll go over that later."

The color of Roger's face faded from crimson to pink as he mulled the problem of extra guards. "Can't your office do it?" he asked.

"We don't have the staff to closely supervise even the Chuparrosa portion of your development. The county police will come if you have a problem, but you can't count on them for patrols."

"Would four more be enough?" he pondered, frowning. "They're going to be expensive. We've got to think about the bottom line here."

"And well worth it, if you can prevent vandalism." Sanchez said. "I'll talk to my deputies and try to find out how the water group feels about things. If there's any hint of mischief, we'll follow up, but we've got no crystal ball. Your additional patrols could well pay for themselves in prevention."

"Right," Roger growled. "Pella, get out the list of guard companies and order four beginning tonight. Anything else?"

"Don't fire Ben until we find out how the computer's were reprogrammed," Sanchez suggested. "It probably wasn't his fault."

"I'll give him twenty-four hours," Roger barked and hoisted his heavy frame out of the chair. "You find out who did that, and we'll prosecute 'em! Come on, Ford, let's get back to the big game." He clapped the smaller man on the shoulder and launched him toward the door. "Oh, uh, take care of yourself, Pella," he mumbled as he stepped into the sunshine.

Pella frowned at their retreating figures. "What a lovable guy my employer is! Too bad I'm not quite as valuable as his beautiful green grass."

"He's counting on me to take care of you, *cara mía,* and I can if you'll do what I say." He made an effort to keep his manner easy. He wasn't encouraged by the stubborn look in her eyes. "What's your daily schedule?"

"I get here at 8:30. Usually Roger checks in, makes phone calls, dictates e-mails and letters. By 10:00 he's off to the corporate headquarters in the Valley or taking VIPs on tours. I stay until 12:30, answering phones, doing office work, helping realtors with their clients."

"You're sometimes alone between 8:30 and 12:30?"

"Hey, it's a gated community. We don't get walk-in traffic. The local realtors and Greenwood Development staff show the homes and lots, then make the sales. The contractors' crews go to their own work sites. I sit here in lonely splendor for four hours, with my nose to the grindstone."

"Then you drive from here to the town hall and eat your lunch in the courtyard?"

"I have been known to pick up a sandwich at the Croissant as I drive through town, but it's not a pattern. I stay at the town hall office until five or six. After that, I have festival meetings, or even," Pella grinned, "the occasional date."

Hank stood, hands in his pockets, jingling his change, wondering how he could protect her as he wanted to without goading her to rebellion. He had no right to demand she catch the first plane to Cabos San Lucas and stay there until the threat to her life was over.

She watched him worry for a while. "You can't be with me every minute, Hank," she said. "You'd be a fool to try."

"Well, how about this?" he said at last. "I'll drive behind you from your place to this office about eight in the morning. Keep the doors here locked. The gate attendant will notify you if some authorized person needs to come in. The patrol will swing by at 12:30 and escort you to the town hall. There you'll be within shouting distance. For the next few days, plan to stay in your office and do your errands on the phone." He cleared his throat. "After working hours, I'll be in charge."

"Hank, I'm not going to stay at your place."

He shrugged. "Then you'll have to wear a security lavaliere."

"Like old Mrs. Winchell wears?"

"No, bigger than that. With a battery that sounds an alarm when you set it off"

She gave him a withering look. "Bad! Very bad for my image as a healthy, strong, single woman. And what do I say when someone asks me why?"

"Make sure you wear it at home, too. Every place but the shower. And for God's sake, keep the security alarm on in your apartment. And your doors locked."

"Glory always forgets her key." Pella tossed her head. "You're going to a great deal of trouble over some sleazy creature who's probably all bluster."

"That's not a chance I'm willing to take." He tried not to sound pleading. "Come to Casa Amarilla with me after work tonight."

"I have a festival committee meeting at seven. I can't arrive full of margaritas." A flush began to creep over her face again. "And Hank, I won't be big-brothered."

Exasperated, he'd grabbed her arms and kissed her. "Pella," he said, feeling his face harden into a frown, "do this one thing for me. Please. I'll catch this *pinché bastardo* and ship him to Tierra del Fuego, but for the next week, *en el nombre de Dios,* take a few damn orders!"

Chapter 6

"Let's carry our chairs out on the colonnade," Patsy Hegerty urged as she squeezed into Pella's tiny Festival Planning Office in the town hall quadrangle and stepped over Charlie Talaferro's long legs to an empty folding seat. "There's a moon tonight. No chance of more rain."

"Too hot," Charlie grumbled. "Can we start the meeting? I've got to get back to the saloon. Pete's on a camping trip, and I've got Jeremiah Morley behind the bar." He squirmed on the metal chair and smoothed a restless finger over the moustache that drooped around his mouth. "That boy's a competent bar tender, but he's got a quick temper like all the Morleys. More muscles than sense."

"Sure." Pella smiled and hitched up the shoulder of her gray knit dress, aware that Charlie was having trouble keeping his eyes off the neckline. She wished she'd made Hank drive her to her place so she could have changed into jeans and a shirt. And, damn it, she'd let him talk her into leaving her car there, too, so now she was dependent on him for a ride home. She was beginning to feel like a pizza, being delivered everywhere.

Most of her festival committee chairmen had gathered as ordered. Patsy Hegerty, parade, and Bud Brickson, old settlers' picnic, were with Charlie, rodeo, in the front row of chairs. Shy Zephyr Wilson, concert, huddled in the back against the window.

"Maud and Sugar are the only ones missing." Pella grinned at her team. "Maud's coming when she can break away from rehearsals.

46

Zephyr tells me Sugar has a sick horse and has to wait for the vet. What's new with the rodeo, Charlie?"

Charlie settled one tooled leather boot on the other knee and balanced a tattered spiral notebook on top of it. He was dressed in his summer uniform – T-shirt and blue jeans worn to a ghostly white down the thighs. His leather belt and generous commemorative buckle were nearly obscured by the bulge that appeared when he slouched. A cowboy hat, wide and crisp, reposed beneath his chair.

"We have a hundred and five entries, but a bunch'll come in at the last minute. Cowboy's are like that," he said, ticking off the items with his finger. "We got a work party to patch up the arena last week, and we'll have plenty of room for horse trailers around it. Spools of tickets are ready. I've found animals for the bull, bronco and calf events. Exhibitors have rented booths to sell hats and leather goods. The Baptist ladies'll have a nacho and pop booth. The Legion'll have hotdogs and beer. They'll also take care of any food sale permits." He gave Pella a wink and scratched the eagle tattoo just above his wrist. "So what else?"

"Uh—Charlie, PA system?" Pella prompted. "Porta-potties?"

"Oh, yeah." His grin drooped. "I still gotta do that."

"Do it tomorrow, Charlie. We can't have a rodeo way out at the arena without those things. The customers expect more than megaphones and bushes."

"There aren't that many bushes out there, anyway," Charlie noted as he planted his boots firmly on the floor. His eyes, under shaggy brows, begged permission to leave. "Sure. Tomorrow."

Charlie always surprised Pella. He was an exemplary citizen of Chuparrosa, working hard on civic committees. The gentleness and commitment didn't quite jibe with his wild-pirate appearance and the boisterous saloon he owned. Nobody knew much about his past. He kept whatever animals were within him tightly reined.

"Have you located an announcer we can afford? And volunteers to help with livestock and parking? What about prize money? Programs?" She gave him an encouraging smile, hating to nag.

"Clint Smith from Holbrook will announce, and I'll help him. I've got a signup sheet at the saloon for volunteers. And nobody gets out of there without signin' up." Charlie scowled. "We'll use the entrance fees for prize money and the gate receipts for expenses. Programs'll go to press on Monday, the cutoff day for entries." The big man shifted again in his folding chair and glanced at the clock. "Permission to vamoose, senorita. Jeremiah screws up when things get hectic."

"Your customers start fighting at a quarter of eight on Thursday nights?" Bud Brickson asked with a grin.

"Jerry can't manage the popcorn machine." Charlie gave his head a puzzled shake. "The guys get kinda violent if we run out of popcorn." He smiled at Pella. "I'll take care of the PA and the potties tomorrow. Don't sweat it."

"Talk about relief!" She watched him sweep his hat off the floor, stretch to his full six-three and amble out the door. A graceful man, Pella thought. He moved on the balls of his feet like a dancer. She knew he'd be embarrassed if she ever mentioned it.

"Pella, we've had quite a time digging out old settlers," Bud complained. His hands rested on knobby knees that jutted below his plaid shorts. "Most have moved to California to live with their kids."

His brown eyes goggled at her behind thick lenses, and his baldhead, atop a narrow fringe of white hair, glistened like pink plastic in the overhead lights. A retired insurance man from the east coast, he'd come to Arizona for year-round golf. He looked frail, but bounced along with surprising energy. During the winter social season, Bud played Don Juan, squiring a variety of willing widows.

"Some of our old settlers in Valley nursing homes are too feeble to attend, or I guess they'd move to California, too. So far we have twelve who're still ambulatory and have relatives or friends to bring 'em. Nine ladies and three gentlemen." Bud glanced up from his notes, grinning. "We've even found a couple of ranch hands from the old time Cloud Builder Ranch north of town and a realtor, Pete Rivers, who still live here. We'll present each one with a small corsage or boutonniere and a certificate acknowledging their fifty-plus years in our community."

"Should we honor the younger people who've lived in Chuparrosa for at least thirty years?" Pella asked. "Sugar and Butch Morley have lived on their place that long."

"Yes, well, we've invited the whole town to apply for the limited reservations, but the elderly guests don't pay for their dinners. If we had too many, we couldn't afford 'em. The picnic's being catered by St. Elizabeth's Parish ladies." He scanned his notes. "The usual. Fried chicken, fruit salad, baked beans, rolls and cake. Lots of iced tea and pop."

"Held here in the courtyard?"

"Right. That's why we can only cram in 100. We rented tables and chairs, and we'll clean up everything afterwards. Make sure the mayor's here, Pella. He's supposed to give a welcoming speech. Our local historian, Laura Pritchard, will offer a short program, and everyone will be able to renew old friendships. Since there's no honorarium for Laura in our budget, we'll let her sell her history of Chuparrosa."

"Sounds good, Bud." Pella nodded, frowning at her notes. The mayor would be no problem. He was up for re-election in November, and he liked nothing better than giving welcoming speeches. "You've made a reservation for Claire Tubbs? We want plenty of space in the Hummer."

"The press lady's promised to attend and bring her camera." Bud peeled his damp knit shirt off the back of the folding chair and strolled toward the door, fumbling in his pocket.

"You're coming back, aren't you?" Pella asked and then caught herself. She'd suffered through another of Hank's brain-washings during their hurried dinner at Casa Amarilla. It had made her jumpy. This new fear that followed her throughout the day settled its icy hands on her shoulders once more. She braced herself to fight it. "But you don't have to, of course, unless you want to."

"Just going for a smoke." Bud raised his pointed eyebrows. "I'll stay for the whole meeting."

"I've got to be next, Pella." Patsy Hegerty's squeaky voice shrilled in her ear. "Sean and Shawna will be out of pageant rehearsal by 8:30.

The Little Coyotes practice early since it's a school night. Shirlene Watson runs them through their dance three times this week because we're getting so close to the first performance. They are just adorable."

"Okay, Patsy, how's the parade coming?"

"Oh, great!" Patsy's polished nails began to flip through the forms in her three-ring notebook. "We have over a hundred entries. A few are one-horse equestrian units, of course, but we also have floats and bands and marching children." She glanced up to include Zephyr in her excitement. "The Shrine mini-cars are coming. And most of the floats will toss things."

"Toss things?" Pella said in alarm.

"Sure. Candy, balloons, little toys. Seventeen local businesses are constructing floats. Great community spirit! Marshal Sanchez promised to help with the traffic detours, and his deputies will be working all day, plus a volunteer posse." She laid a list of names on Pella's desk. "Hank's going to line up the parade on side streets Saturday morning starting at 6:30 and funnel them onto the parade route." Patsy simpered slyly at Pella. "He's been wonderful."

Oh, God, small towns! Pella fumed, trying to ignore Patsy's meaning. She made a note to double-check it all with Hank. The routing system was crucial to the success of the parade, and Patsy was a well-intentioned airhead.

The door opened, and Maud Florence wafted among them, surrounded by hot outside air and heavy perfume. Her white hair drooped into her lavender eyes, darkly penciled, lashes sticky with mascara. The backpack she had slung over her shoulder overflowed with papers. With one hand she clutched the figure-concealing purple dress that billowed about her orthopedic oxfords. Bud followed in her wake.

"I do not have time to come to meetings, Pella, dear, I really do not," Maud pronounced in her professional actress voice. "We will never get this pageant together if I have to skip out on the rehearsals." She dropped into a vacant chair, spilling bits of paper from her bag onto the floor and aimed a piercing whisper into Patsy's ear. "Little Sean and Shawna are waiting for you, dear."

Sean and Shawna's mother gasped and leaped to her feet, tripping over Bud's Adidas in her hurry to escape. "Call me if you need me, Pella." she squealed as she disappeared into the muggy darkness.

"Zephyr," Pella said to the young woman huddled on a chair beneath the window, "do you mind if we hear from Maud first? You've been waiting a long time, I know, but…"

Zephyr came out of her daze with a start and shook her head. "That's all right. I'm not in any hurry."

Not in any hurry to get back to the bully she lives with, Pella thought. Their bouts of domestic violence often made the police reports in the Chuparrosa Hummer. If the fights grew too noisy to ignore, neighbors called the marshal to the rented house on Spanish Saddle Mountain where Zephyr and her boy friend, Jake Scarlett, lived. The man spared her face, but when hot weather called for tank tops, Zephyr couldn't conceal the bruises on her arms.

Maud pressed a handkerchief to one temple and then the other. "God, it is hot! Do you have any ice water, my dear?"

Bud got to his feet. "I'll get you some pop from the machine, Maud. Anyone else?"

Her face crinkled into a smile. "Well, if you are going. Something white, please. I can only stay a minute. I have promised to work with the sheep ranchers from nine to ten. Since I created all the choreography, I have to oversee the rehearsals. I wrote down the steps for the dancing palo verde trees, however, so Peter can rehearse them while I am gone." She tucked back a dangling strand of hair. "They are truly precious."

Pella had been delighted to inherit Maud along with the chairmanship of the Festival Committee. An old timer by Chuparrosa standards, she'd watched the town evolve for twenty-five years, from a dusty village to a fashionable destination for wealthy winter visitors. It was her idea to dramatize the story of gold miners Thunder Grogen and Alfred Schlund, who had been the first residents of the town 125 years ago. Fired by her own enthusiasm, she'd written a script, advertised for a cast, and proceeded to produce and direct the pageant. The whole community had come alive in this elderly dynamo's fervor, and people of all ages were now amazed to find themselves dancing, prancing, singing and acting on the stage of the high school auditorium. All Pella had to do was stand back and let her do it.

Maud raised her violet eyes to Bud as he laid the pop can in her lap. "Bless you, sir," she breathed, and rolled the icy metal across her forehead, eyes closed, lips parted.

"What has to be done before opening night, Maud, and how can I help?" Pella asked, trying to move the lady along.

"Find me an extra week, Pella," she begged. "We will never be ready in ten days."

"Nothing easier. But is one enough? How about two or three?"

Looking bewildered, Maud pulled the tab on her pop can and took a sip. "Do not tease me, Pella. I am a serious person with serious needs. The lighting on that school stage is atrocious!"

"Why don't I dig up the head custodian, and we'll meet you over there—say tomorrow afternoon? We'll get their lighting expert there, too. You can tell them exactly what you require, and they can arrange to take care of it." Bravely said, she thought. The lighting and sound is undoubtedly technical. Count on the custodian to be an old grouch who'll drive Maud into spasms.

"Oh, Pella," the lady sighed, "that would be marvelously helpful. My late husband used to say, 'if you can not depend on a beautiful blond, who can you depend on?'"

A blast of stifling air swept into the room again as Sugar Morley, out of breath, gray curls bobbing, darted through the door. She wore cutoff jeans, the raveled edges tickling her thighs, a T-shirt extolling the virtues of Howling Coyote Feeds and the fine country smell of horses and stable. Sugar had been a saucy young woman once. She still moved with grace, her actions denying any changes the years had brought. From a distance, Pella thought, with her youthful figure she could pass for thirty, but her skin had been coarsened and lined by years of curing in the Arizona sun. Closer inspection betrayed her age.

The most startling features in Sugar's permanently tanned face were her eyes. The irises, a shining aquamarine, glittered like the transparent water that filled Chuparrosa's swimming pools. She shunned makeup, but her eyes, pale turquoise and white, had a magnetic clarity that riveted attention.

Pushing her way back beside Zephyr, Sugar patted the girl's shoulder. "Hi, kid," she said, and then addressed the others. "Sorry I'm late. The vet just left. Nothing serious, but when it's a client's horse…" She left the statement up in the air, expecting anyone living in ranch country to understand.

"You're timing's perfect, Sugar. We're almost ready for you," Pella said. "Maud, do you want to go back to the rehearsal? We'll get together at the high school tomorrow at 5:00 and talk about any other problems then. I'll set up the appointment with the lighting man."

"Lovely!" Maud sprang to her feet, broadcasting the heavy scent of lavender among them. "Farewell, sweet things," she called over her shoulder, as she jogged out the door.

Pella breathed a sigh. Just two more to go. "Okay, Zephyr. Let's hear about the concert. Any glitches?"

The girl extracted a sheet of paper from her backpack and cleared her throat. "Uh—the band has been – like rehearsing in the Legion building for a month. It's made up of—like local musicians, and some—uh—like high school students, all under the direction of Elmer Bird. He's a retired band director from Des Moines." Zephyr's weightless voice apologized. Each phrase was a question. "They'll—like—play afternoon concerts, Friday and Saturday in the plaza near the fountain on Gold Dust Road."

She paused to sneak a glance at the others and appeared startled to find they were watching her. Her eyes widened, she blinked and cleared her throat again. "Um—um—it'll be—like old timey stuff—oompah stuff—and they'll dress in white shirts and bow ties, so it'll seem like an old fashioned concert. The drummer will wear a fake mustache."

"Great job, Zephyr!"

"It was pretty easy," the girl confessed. "I just called Elmer Bird, and he did the rest. Jeremiah and Micah Morley'll—um like—help me haul those white plastic chairs for the band on Friday morning. We'll like stack 'em in the back room at the Balloon 'N Ballyhoo shop after like each concert." Her anxious eyes checked Pella's face. Her fingers trembled as she reached across Bud with the report.

"Good! I can't wait to hear them play. You're on top of everything," Pella said, lathering on positive reinforcement. Her efforts to boost Zephyr's self-esteem hadn't been a brilliant success. Any friendly lures had yet to penetrate her cloud of shyness. "The photos of the band rehearsing will be featured in the Festival program. You've hit every mark, Zephyr. I wish everyone was so well organized."

The girl stood up, pulled down the thigh length skirt, and adjusted her sleeveless sweater. The bruise on her thin shoulder winked purple and yellow as she bent to pick up her backpack. Whatever Sugar whispered to her at that moment made her face flame. "There—there wasn't anything much to do," she repeated, turning away. Uh— g'night." She opened the door a few inches, squeezed her skinny frame out into the courtyard and closed it again, with no sound.

"Arts and crafters!" Pella sang out. Maybe they could wind this up before ten so she could go home and try to forget the whole worrisome day. "How many have you found, Sugar?"

The open smile that Sugar fixed on Zephyr's retreating figure vanished when she swung around to Pella. A sullen, hard stare took its place. "I've got fifty-three exhibitors. They'll set up their booths in the patios and plazas along Gold Dust, out of the way of the parade. Space assignments have all been made."

"They're bringing their own equipment, right?"

"Tents or stalls, eight by ten feet."

Pella raised her head as she heard the tone of the innocent statement that contained a clear challenge. Sugar's turquoise eyes gleamed ominously. Mystified, Pella wondered what she'd done. She and Sugar hadn't become buddies over the past few months, but they'd gotten along all right. Bud was staring at Sugar with a puzzled frown on his face.

"Would you like me to find more cleanup people for you?" Were there enough volunteers in the whole town, she wondered, to clean up all the Festival messes?

"I have my friends up on the Mountain to help," Sugar said. The words "friends" and "Mountain" were emphasized, walling off the rest of Chuparrosa. The bitterness in her voice slashed like a razor.

"Got any of those pottery people coming to the show?" Bud made an attempt to deflect the darts falling around Pella. For him, Sugar's face bloomed in a genuine smile. He lived near the bottom of her mountain, a "fringie," but still a Spanish Saddle Mountain person.

"Thirteen potters, coming from as far away as Nogales and Winslow," Sugar announced. "The State Wildlife Conservancy is going to have a booth. So is our local Land Trust." She flung a defiant glare at Pella, who finally grasped the fact that the Morleys had cast her as a villain, exploiting water needed by people on the Mountain.

"Sugar," she began, "I'm not your enemy. I'm truly not. We can't be choosing up sides here."

Sugar's scowl grew more glacial. "You've already chosen. You work for Sonoran Skyline. You're the ones who're stealing our water, our livelihood, our legacy for our children. As long as you've got that job, you're one of them."

The hatred in her tone made Pella blink. "In ten days I'll lose this job." She waved her hand around the cramped office. "I have to eat, too. Be realistic."

There was triumph in the sneer that disfigured Sugar's tan face. "Then move in with that Mexican marshal you're sleeping with. If he puts his hands on me again, he'll be sorry. My boys don't let anyone manhandle their mama."

She cast a quick glance at Bud, who stared at her, his face pink with embarrassment. "I just came tonight to warn you and Sanchez. You'd both better get on the right side of this battle, or you'll be among the missing in action."

She kicked the metal chairs out of her way making them clatter, brushed past Bud and lunged for the door. Her mouth formed a startled "O" when she collided in the doorway with Hank Sanchez. "Don't touch me, you bastard!" Sugar spit the words out, ducked to one side, as if to avoid a blow, and dashed for her pickup.

Pella covered her eyes with her hands, blocking off the anger that rippled through the room.

Hank's calm voice asked, "What's going on?"

Bud chortled, "Sugar's not so sweet tonight."

Then she was aware of Hank's fingers massaging the back of her neck, and feeling the strength in his hand, risked observing the world again.

Bud, fists stuffed into the pockets of his baggy shorts, shifted from one foot to the other, staring at Sanchez. "Those twenty horses at Sugar's drink a lot of water, and I've heard her well's about dry. The whole Spanish Saddle Mountain crowd have decided you're part of the trouble, I guess. They figure they'll have better luck fighting Town Hall than Greenwood Development."

"The town has a lot more sympathy for them," Hank agreed. He smiled at Pella, an intimate, white-toothed flash of charm that lit up all the empty spaces inside her like the sudden catch of a mesquite fire.

She started scooping papers back into her file, tidying the desk, aware that Bud was studying them, guessing Sugar was right about the marshal being her lover. Five months ago she'd established the friendship-only ground rules with Hank and held him to it. But those smiles, even more dangerous than his kisses, threatened to buckle the mettle of her resolve.

Her goal was emotional independence. She refused to indulge in a parasitic alliance where Hank provided the strength, and she sucked it up. Whatever albatross the marshal hung around his neck, she would make sure it wasn't Pella VanDoren.

She swung her purse onto her shoulder. "That's it for tonight, guys. Bud, could you possibly give me a ride home?"

Bud shot Hank a baffled look. "Well, I...sure, if...?"

While the question hung between the two men, Pella strode to the door and stepped out onto the darkened patio. "Marshal, please turn off the lights and pull the door shut when you leave," she said. Then she turned her back on them and headed toward Bud's red Mercedes convertible parked by the curb. If living her life freely meant taking the chance of meeting that snarly-voiced creature in some dark alley, well—she'd just have to risk it.

Chapter 7

Hank Sanchez turned his patrol car into the shade of a palo verde tree at the top of the curving driveway that snaked up to Fiesta Flores's adobe home. He stepped out, inhaling air heavy with the scent of burrsage and creosote bushes. From where he stood near the top of Spanish Saddle Mountain, he could look north and west, across an endless succession of ridges to Crown King, jutting up like a brooding mirage on the far horizon. This was an exclusive area, few houses, few roads. The only noises were the contented sounds of Fiesta's animals, thoroughbred horses, several dogs of various sizes, a couple of goats, peacocks and fancy chickens, and the muted clang of bells as their clappers swung in the breeze.

Fiesta had set her house in the center of her five acres. Its flamboyant style, known locally as mock-mission, boasted the full repertoire of Southwestern architecture—arches, balustrades, niches occupied by Santos, bell towers, wrought iron balconies, colonnades and a carved stone fountain. The stable and dog run lay on the other side of the house, screened by ocotillos and yuccas. He noticed the fountain wasn't bubbling and splashing as it had been on other visits. Only a few inches of brackish liquid lapped at the white ring that encrusted its bowl. Even a recycling fountain couldn't work without some water.

Fiesta's expensive layout on the top of the mountain had all been paid for by her career as a Spanish dancer, her fiery flamenco footwork performed to gypsy rhythms. Magazine articles about her claimed she'd made her debut as a child in New Mexico with such glowing success that at sixteen she'd stopped being plain Maria Cruz, quit school and formed a dancing troop of her own. She still traveled with her dancers as star performer, but much of her energy now went into the school she'd founded to train students in flamenco. Shrewd at business as well as her art, she'd invested her profits in Arizona real estate, and made a bundle.

Hank pushed his way through the wooden gate in the patio wall and followed a stone path into the shade of an arched colonnade that ran the length of the house. A cactus wren, perched on the wall, squawked in alarm as he approached the door. Sanchez grinned. Nature's warning of possible pitfalls in dealing with Fiesta? Experience had made him fully aware of the risks. He pulled the bell rope.

A child-sized woman flung the door open. The loose rose-colored dress she wore hung almost to her sandals. Its square embroidered neck and short sleeves revealed the plumpness of her arms and shoulders. Her dark hair was coiled into a bun at the base of her neck.

"Buenos dias, senor mariscal," she cooed, tipping her head back to look into Hank's face.

"¿Como esta usted, Senora Gutierrez?" He and Fiesta's housekeeper were old friends. She was always glad to see anyone who didn't make her struggle with English. Fiesta had lured her from her village in the mountains north of Santa Fe when the house was new, but her second language had not improved over the years. She sputtered in rapid Spanish to Chuparrosa shopkeepers, sprinkling in a few ill-chosen English nouns as rewards she felt they did not deserve. Privately she vowed that she couldn't understand why they were all so *muy estúpido*.

"La senorita is in the patio getting ready to swim." She spun around and flicked her fingers, beckoning him to follow her through the house, her heavy thighs undulating beneath the dress as she rocked from side to side. "She has had a ride on her favorite horse, Conquistador, and drunk her coffee, so now she swims and in a while she will go teach the ladies and gentlemen at the dancing school."

Ceiling fans whirled rivulets of air around the cool room. Through the open patio doors Sanchez could see Fiesta standing in a halo of sunlight, reflected from the pool's turquoise water. Her dark hair tumbled over her shoulders. Shapely tanned legs showed below her knee-length robe. You're here on business, he told himself, so keep your mind on it. Another cactus wren scolded from the top of a saguaro as Fiesta threw back her head and warmed him with a smile.

"Café con leche, Juana," she ordered, taking his arm and leading him into the shade of the overhang where two leather chairs stood beside a small table. The older woman, stirring the air as only a woman of her girth can, bustled into the depths of the house. Fiesta sank into one of the chairs and waved Hank to the other, giving him a look that implied more intimacy than they had so far shared. "How nice to have breakfast coffee with you," she murmured.

Sanchez pulled a notebook and pencil from his shirt pocket to underline his official capacity. "I'm glad you could see me this morning," he said, plowing into his mission. "This water committee business has me worried. Folks up here on the Mountain may have valid reasons to be angry, but malicious mischief is against the law, and I have to check it all out."

A breeze freshened the ripples on the pool. Fiesta stared across to the mountains, quiet in the hazy distance. "I'm glad to see you anytime, Hank," she said in a compliant voice. "For any reason."

He waited to see if she continued, but her gaze was fixed on the horizon, so he pressed ahead. "I see the committee has pickets across from the gates to Sonoran Skyline this morning. You're not with them on that, are you?"

"Mostly weekends," she said, smoothing the ties on her robe along one thigh with her hand. "I'm a working girl."

Juana appeared with a tray of coffee, milk in a jug and two earthenware mugs. She set it on the table, giggled and went away. Fiesta reached over to pour. *"¿Con leche para ti?"* she purred, and added milk when he nodded.

"Is there a chairman? Who's calling the shots, planning agendas?" Hank picked up the cup and inhaled the fragrance. Juana Gutierrez made outstanding coffee.

"Will you join me for a swim in a little while?" she asked, scooping a hand through her black hair.

Hank set down his mug. "Fiesta, nothing would be more pleasant than to sit on your patio and pass the time of day over coffee, but like you, I have to work. And I'm trying to work right now." He frowned, making an effort to read her mind. "If you don't intend to answer my questions, I'll be on my way."

She gave her shoulders a sulky shake, her eyes back on the mountains. "Enrique, will you never put aside business for pleasure?" she muttered in Spanish. "You lead such a meager life."

"And you will greatly enrich it with your answers. Who's heading up the water committee?"

"Sugar Morley wants to tell us what to do and so far we've been going along with her ideas, but Bud Brickson's afraid the Morleys are too radical. Sugar may have reason to be, though, since the shortage of water puts her business in jeopardy. Anyway, she's organizing the pickets, and she and her boys promised to make signs. I doubt very much if Jerry and Micah wrote the words. I think they're both illiterate."

"Will you be meeting weekly, daily?"

"Every Thursday night at Bud's."

"What does Bud want to do?"

Fiesta laughed. "Old Bud is so law-abiding. He's planning a petition drive and a letter-writing campaign and setting up meetings with the state water board. I can't tell you how we're energized by his plodding industry."

"Who killed Roger Martineau's dog, Fiesta?" Hank asked. "An intruder climbed onto their patio and drowned Curly in the family pool on the night of the water forum at town hall."

She set down her mug. "I don't understand. You mean some guy held a dog under water until it drowned?"

"That's right. We found a package of meat in the patio. Someone climbed the wall, made friends with Curly and left his body in the pool." Hank studied her reaction. He wasn't surprised to see that she looked upset. "What's the gossip among your neighbors? And how about the reprogramming of the sprinklers at Sonoran Skyline so they went off during the golf tournament yesterday?" Hank hesitated, wanting her to know the seriousness of the actions, but not all the details. "Or threatening someone with death?"

"Death! Oh, come on, Hank. This is just a neighborly group up here. We haven't killed anybody for at least a week. My only contact with the committee, since a ten-minute rally after the water forum, was a phone call from Sugar about picketing. She got ugly when I refused to close my school and participate today." Fiesta reached out for the coffee pot and refilled their mugs, splashing a puddle on the tray in her haste. She raised one delicate eyebrow. "So who's been threatened?"

He ignored her question. No point in being drawn into any crossfire. "No one has been gloating over Martineau's dog?"

"Don't be stupid! We all have dogs of our own. A lot of folks up here prefer dogs to people. No one considers this a killing matter, anyway." She stared at her coffee mug. "Well, maybe Sugar does," she said, half to herself. "Maybe her boys. Their place has a second mortgage. I suppose they could lose it if they have to go on hauling water. And they've been up here on the mountain so long, they have stone feet."

"Could Sugar or her boys have broken into the golf lodge and reprogrammed the sprinkler system?"

"Jerry and Micah? They wouldn't know how," Fiesta snapped. "And they would have taken pot shots at Roger before they'd harm his dog." She uncoiled her legs, stood up on bare feet and came around the table to bend over him, leaning her hands on the arms of his chair. "Come swimming with me, *pobre monje, Enrique*." She brought her smiling red mouth down on his, lips soft, welcoming.

It was a long kiss, offering hours of bright pleasure now and in the future. He enjoyed it more than he wanted her to know. Thoughts of what could have been his attacked him with sudden vigor. Hands against her shoulders, he pushed her back reluctantly, his heart pounding as she straightened up,

"Trying to enrich my meager life?" he asked, in a shaky voice.

"My civic duty." Fiesta moved to the pool, her back to him. With one flowing motion, she unzipped the robe, letting it drop to the deck, and with a flash of well-toned buttocks and breasts, made a shallow dive into the water.

Sanchez stared, aware for the first time that she'd been stark naked under the robe, and cried *"¡Bravissimo!"* No woman had ever put on a show quite like that for him. *"Senorita,* I'm honored," he breathed. Then he was on his feet and lunging for the door before she came up for air, golden shoulders and black hair glistening with drops of water like diamonds. The Spanish she flung at his retreating figure contained shrill and pointed remarks concerning both his lineage and his manhood.

Hank quick-timed it to the patrol car, squelching the aching regrets for missed opportunities. With a valiant effort, he turned his mind back to the water business. A breeze flowed down the back slope of the mountain, cooling his head, if not his ardor. He wiped his brow, beat back the fantasies and tried to think about what he had to do next.

There was the matter of the break-in at the Sonoran Skyline's golf lodge. Yesterday afternoon's investigation of the scene of that incident had Sanchez and his deputy Rhys Jones still scratching their heads. They found none of the usual signs of a forced entry, the jimmied door, the broken window, damage to the roof. The fingerprints all belonged to staff members, who insisted nothing was missing or even rearranged. The burglar had probably arrived silently on foot, but left no prints on the short-cropped grass or the textured sidewalk. The keys to the building were all accounted for. Ben Talbot, the course manager, swore that his staff had used the same watering program for the past two hot months and hadn't touched the computers. Angry Roger Martineau agreed to keep Ben on a trial basis for another month.

At the moment their offender appeared to be a clean, tidy computer whiz, who wore gloves, wiped his feet and was thin enough to slide under doors. Maybe Sugar knew something about that.

The Morley's place lay below Fiesta's, to the south, overlooking the valley. He might as well stop in to see her on his way to town. She'd been angry last night when they'd collided at Pella's office. He hoped to find her in a calmer mood this morning.

Sanchez drove along the gravel road that was the thoroughfare around the mountain, his car leaving a spiraling coil of dust hanging in the air. Every year the town offered to blacktop Apache Boot Wash Road, and every year the folks living on Spanish Saddle refused the offer. The residents considered their property rural and their five to ten acre lots small ranches. Only a gravel road secured that status. Its rocks and ruts discouraged casual traffic. Privacy was important. If you saw a cloud of dust blowing into your open windows, you liked to think it was from your neighbor's pickup, not the Cadillac of some tourist from New Jersey.

Morley's Apache Boot Stables stood closer to the road than Fiesta's home. The short driveway brought Hank's patrol car into a parking area against the back of the stable. Sugar could provide either box stalls, tucked away inside the cool interior of the barn, or breezy open stalls, consisting of a tin roof divided by tubular fencing. Between the two stall areas was a spacious exercise paddock thick with reddish dust, a powdery cushion for delicate legs.

Two arenas took up nearly all the rest of the Morley's five acres – one for jumping and one for western riding. Any leftover land around the edges could be used for trail riding across the desert. The horses Sugar kept in her stable were year-round boarders, though their owners stayed only the nine months from October to May. She kept her fifteen equine guests healthy and active during the summer so they'd be fit for their owners to ride in the fall.

Hank knew Sugar managed her business only by long, hot hours of training, grooming, feeding and mucking out. For years, the operation had been the chief support of the family. Jeremiah worked as Charlie's brawny bartender, and Micah helped out at the Howling Coyote Feed Store. Her husband, Butch, did odd jobs, when he could be motivated. Most Chuparrosans agreed that Sugar had all the brains and spunk in the bunch.

The desert climate had taken its toll on the ranch buildings, including the Morley home, situated beyond the stable. Paint peeled from the wood frame of the front porch and bare black spots showed on the roof where green pebbles, glued on years before, had come loose and rolled to the ground. Everything cried for attention, Sanchez noticed. Sugar couldn't do it all.

He opened the car door and moved his long frame out from under the steering wheel. Two dogs, a collie and a black lab, swarmed about his legs, making no commotion, sniffing and pressing their noses into his hands. Out of the corner of his eye he was aware that a curtain twitched on a front window of the house, but Sugar, chaps tied over shorts, was in the jumping arena exercising a flashy bay mare. No point in going to the house to see Butch Morley, a sullen guy who'd made it plain on several occasions that he had little use for Hispanics.

The dogs, knowing their places, left Hank at the paddock. He cut between the two stables, past the gleaming hindquarters and swishing tails of the horses, and made his way along the aisle to stand beside the arena. Sugar, collecting the horse into a canter, circled the ring. She glared at him each time they passed and at last pulled the mare to a halt beside him, making her take shorter and shorter steps until the horse stopped, ears pricked, feet set neatly together.

"Wow! A prize winning performance, Sugar." He ran his hand down the mare's blaze. "That's a beautiful sight to see."

The hard look on Sugar's face softened for an instant and then re-formed, mouth a straight line, aqua marine eyes glinting in the shade of her hat brim. She seemed smaller perched on top of the big animal, but in perfect control. The gray curls, forming a fringe below her hat, bristled with vitality and confidence.

"What do you want?" she demanded. She switched the whip into her outside hand and began snapping it aggressively against her leather chaps.

"Why aren't you with the pickets?"

Her eyes narrowed. "So you wanted to snoop around here when you thought I was gone."

"Butch is usually here." Sanchez set his boot on one of the cavelleti that circled the ring. "You and I need to talk."

Sugar glanced uneasily toward the house and then back at Hank, flicking a fly off her boot with the whip. The mare twitched her ears, but stood still. "I'm working. And then I have to go back to the pickets after lunch. We're going to stay there across the road from Sonoran Skyline until that s.o.b. turns his sprinklers off for good. And there's not a damn thing you can do to stop us."

"Well, maybe you'll get some action that way." Sanchez shrugged. "I hope none of your crowd suffers heat stroke. I'm surprised at the illegal acts you and your group have been committing, though. Drowning Roger's dog was cruel, a waste of time and a life."

"Serves him right," Sugar shot back. "Our animals are suffering up here because he's taking our water. We have to rent tanks and have it trucked in to replace what he's stealing from us."

"Reprogramming the sprinkler system was a burglary, Sugar. That's a felony."

She fingered the reins a moment before she spoke. "The water committee had nothing to do with either of those things. We're picketing, writing letters and petitioning the water board. That's all."

"Even if you're not doing it yourselves, you know who is. You must approve of the rough stuff. Is it just you, or does the whole committee believe in breaking the law?"

"We believe in getting what's rightfully ours!"

"The mayor and the council are scrambling to come up with some way of supplying you with water out here."

"Oh, sure they are. And we'll all die of thirst before that happens! Mel Bergen is a golfer." She spat the word out with all the venom she would have used to say "child molester."

"He cares more for his recreation than for our needs. Our enemies are his big buddies." Sugar's eyes were clear and cold as icebergs. "And what's more you're a tool of that regime."

Sanchez wiped a hand across his brow. The sweat was running between his shoulder blades. Sugar's tank top was soaked. He knew she had to be miserable in those heavy chaps. The mare's head drooped. She flipped her tail at a fly.

"Sugar, I could sure use a drink of water." He grinned up at her. "If you'll jump off that mare and get me one, I'll cool her and put her away. We can talk better in the shade."

She gave a bark of laughter, gathered the reins and straightened her back. Instantly the mare's head came to attention, accepting the bit, moving into a flowing trot.

"Haven't you heard, Marshal?" Sugar shouted, as she swept around the curved end of the ring to the far side. "We've learned to do without the luxury of water up here!"

Chapter 8

Hank pointed his patrol car west, carving back through the dust that hovered over Apache Boot Wash Road. He knew he'd made no headway with Sugar. Worse, he'd asked for her crack about the water. When he pulled up for the stop sign on Buckskin Trail that led to the heart of Chuparrosa, he reached into the back seat, groping for the bottle of water he always carried there. He took a long swig, while he stared at the substantial row of rooftops bordering the fairways at Sonoran Skyline on the opposite side of the road.

The Spanish Saddle Mountain crowd was in a panic, and it was easy to understand why. He knew that even Sugar's simple lifestyle couldn't be sustained for long without water. No lifestyle could. It was no good watching your neighbors below at their country club activities while the investment in your home shriveled in the blazing Arizona sun.

Sanchez set the bottle in the cup holder and turned north toward the entrance to Sonoran Skyline. Across the road from the massive stone gatehouse, a group of listless adults huddled in the porous shade of a mesquite tree. A few braver ones held umbrellas or tried to fold their bodies into the shadows from their sun hats. Coolers of all sizes were heaped in a jumble on the ground. Everybody perked up at the sight of Hank's car and began waving cardboard signs. The unflattering cartoons of Roger Martineau, a few quick, impetuous lines, had been sketched with great skill. Who, Hank wondered, was the talented artist?

He parked on the shoulder of the road near the pickets and strolled toward the closest group. They looked hot and dispirited. Not so strange, given a temperature close to one hundred in the shade. No one in this crowd was young.

"Hi," he said. "How's everybody doin'?"

They eyed him with distrust and muttered half-hearted greetings. Bud Brickson came over, his hand held out, while the others turned their backs and bunched together for solidarity.

"We're doing all right, Marshal." Bud's eyes, behind mirrored sunglasses, were inscrutable. The band on the cowboy hat he wore to cover his baldhead showed a fresh line of sweat. "You aren't here to chase us away, are you?"

"No, just a social call. I wanted to make sure you all have plenty of sunscreen and water. Do you know the symptoms of sunstroke? Headache, dizziness, fatigue? Call the marshal's office if you need any emergency assistance. The patrol car'll swing over to help." Hank studied Bud's face. He seemed to be the friendliest one of the picketers. "I understand you'll be meeting with the state water board."

"We'll give that route a try." Bud shrugged. "Whatever works."

Hank caught a closer glimpse of the red lettering on the sign Bud held. It condemned Roger for despoiling the desert. The cartoon showed him grinning evilly, an uprooted saguaro clutched in each hefty paw. The words were stenciled on in block letters, but the sketch had been cleverly done with hasty strokes.

"Nice work," Sanchez said. "Did you make these, Bud?"

"Sugar brought them. She must have been up most of the night getting them ready. She'll be back on the picket line after she takes care of her horses. Now there is a dedicated lady."

More like a desperate lady, thought Hank. "Do you know who killed Roger's dog, Bud? Or anything about reprogramming the sprinklers at Sonoran Skyline yesterday?" He lifted his broad-brimmed hat and rocked it back in place. The sun, at a little past noon, bore down fiercely. Water mirages, fake puddles, shimmered in low spots up and down the road.

The older man shook his head and stared down at the toes of his boots. "You know all these people, Hank. Every one of them is a solid, animal-loving citizen."

"A citizen who wants the golf course water turned off. Can you think of anyone with more motive?"

"Killing Curly was an act of intimidation. It accomplished nothing. Ditto the sprinkler business. I will stand as guarantor that it wasn't any of us." Bud stole an uncomfortable look over his shoulder at the group whispering under the mesquite. "But if I hear anything at all, Marshal, I'm going to let you know," he muttered and gestured toward the coolers. "You want a can of pop?"

"No thanks, but I'll hold you to your other offer. Keep pouring liquids into these folks so they don't get sick. And be sure to call for help if you need it."

Sanchez stepped back into his patrol car and made a u-turn into the drive that led to the Sonoran Skyline sales office. The gate attendant snapped to attention, pushing the button that opened the elaborate gate, when he saw the marshal's car. Hank threw him a quick salute and continued on the fancy brick street that wound between artful gardens of irrigated native plants. Pella had the phone to her ear when he entered. She waved and kept jotting notes on a pad.

"Any afternoon of that week would be perfect for me," she said. "Wednesday? At 1:30? Ask for Jan Morrison? I'll be there. Thanks." She hung up the phone and flashed Sanchez a breathless smile. Her expression and a bright pink blouse gave her skin a warm glow.

"I'm starting to look for a full time job," she said. "Something with more benefits and a chance for promotion. When the festival is over, I'll be free for interviews in the afternoons."

"Down in the Valley?"

"Lots of people live here and work in town." Pella scooped her purse out of a drawer and stuffed her scribbled notes inside. "More opportunity." She fluffed her hair. "I'm starved. Are you the escort *du jour*?"

"But you're on a track with Sonoran Skyline. You told me they were interviewing here. Roger's going to need you full time in a few weeks when the tourist season starts." He searched her face. "Are you worried about what Sugar said to you last night?"

"I'll—you know—feel better if I make a change. Roger is not the most endearing boss I've ever had. I'll find something that's more fun and pays better." Making the decision seemed to have removed a weight. She was laughing up at him. "If I can persuade Glory to stop buying jewelry, we might even move into a bigger apartment."

He put his hand on her arm. "I'd like to suggest another kind of living set-up."

"Nope." Her eyes dodged his as she jiggled keys out of her purse.

"Okay, *muchacha ingrata,* but I have a present for you." Sanchez held out the gadget he'd brought her. About three inches in diameter and the color of toast, the lavaliere was attached to a short chain that could be hooked around the neck. A bulging disk in the center would shriek in alarm when pressed.

Pella glared at it with distaste. "It's huge," she said. "How can I hide a thing like that under my clothes?"

"Sorry. There has to be a battery in there. Tell people it's a state-of-the-art communication system, part of your job with the town." He fastened it around her neck, and they both stared at the effect before bursting into laughter.

"It's ridiculous!" Pella said, trying to peer down her nose at the devise. "It looks like a big cookie."

"I'll help you glue on some raisins."

"Hank Sanchez, I'll get you for this assault on my reputation as a brave, independent woman," Pella promised as she headed for the door. "Come on. There's something you should see before we go to city hall."

They drove in separate cars to the huge clubhouse, the second of three planned for the development. A stone monster rising on the edge of the Castle Rock Golf Course, the building had been under construction for several months. The dark rock walls soared above five barren acres of desert from which all living vegetation had been stripped away. A plant parking lot stood along the driveway. There, trees and cactuses struggled on in irrigated wooden boxes until they

70

were needed for landscaping, or if dead, were hauled away. The building was ringed with pickups. Inside, masons and carpenters clattered about as they added stones and scaffolding to the walls.

Pella, with Hank following, threaded her way across the dusty ground, around planks and piles of hardened mortar, to enter the deep shade of the ponderous structure. Even without a roof, the building was ten degrees cooler inside.

"They're doing the main fireplace," Pella told him, as she handed him a hardhat. "I think you ought to see this." She nodded to the workmen, their faces powdered with mortar and whispered, "Come over here."

At the far side of what would be the dining hall, the scaffolding was lower. The fireplace, rising from the floor, had grown only above the box that would contain the fire. It was to be an enormous hearth and chimney, big enough, Hank thought, to roast an ox. The rocks were so large that they had to be lifted by a small crane and guided into their nests of mud.

At the moment, all the workmen had paused to watch the crane raise a rock, the biggest one so far, and aim it for a thick bed of mortar over the hand-hewn granite mantelpiece. Burly men stood by on ladders to bury it in place, brushing off unwanted mud, until the rock face with its hypnotic spiral was revealed.

¡Madre de Dios! Agatha Pure Stone's life stone. Sanchez stared at it, a storm of protest churning in his gut. Pella tugged at his arm, and with an effort, he turned his attention to where she pointed. The rest of the shrine lay on the slab floor, each rock bearing the architect's number indicating where it would be set into the wall.

"Roger told me about them this morning," she whispered. "He says the stones will add blessing and the sanction of the ages to the construction. He honestly believes that everyone will be thrilled to have them preserved in the clubhouse. Of course only the members and their guests will be allowed to view the preservation. Scratch Agatha Pure Stone. And they're changing the name in honor of this little PR coup. It's going to be called the Sacred Stone Golf Course and Clubhouse."

¡El pinché ladrón! Sanchez turned his back on the fireplace and marched outside, pitching his hardhat at the bottom of a colonnade. Arms folded, he leaned against his patrol car and waited for Pella to catch up, trying to cool his anger before it erupted. He'd made a vow not to let his emotions get caught up in this business. He'd made it, but God, it was hard to keep.

"Ready to go?" he said when Pella reached his side. "You're starved, and I have phone calls to make."

They bought sandwiches at the Croissant and picnicked on one of the benches in the city hall plaza. It was cooler there. The fountain sparkled in the dappled shade, sending a spray of moisture onto the fairy dusters and Blackfoot daisies. There weren't many people about. Sanchez found himself raging as he chomped on his roast beef in silence, his mind exploring ways to undo Roger's damage. There weren't any.

Pella touched his arm. "I'm sorry, Hank."

He began to gather up the scraps of their picnic. "It's too late to fix. The BLM should have made arrangements for the shrine when the archaeological survey was done. They handed it over to Roger like some damn gift."

Pella looked thoughtful. "I'll check through the files tomorrow and see what I can find. There may have been stipulations on the deed or the survey that were overlooked."

"Do it soon. That mud sets in twenty minutes. Then it'll take dynamite and a lawsuit to get those stones back in their places. Without a lot of community pressure, the mayor and the council won't bother."

They walked to Pella's Festival office, where Hank checked the single closet and made sure she was wearing the security lavaliere.

Laughing, she protested. "I'm steering clear of swimming pools."

"Do you expect criminals to play by the rules? Even their own rules? When are you going home?"

"Seven, at least." Her mouth formed a tight line. "Okay, I'll let you know."

* * *

Back at his own desk, Sanchez dialed Martineau's number, counted the rings and was amazed when he got the busy man himself instead of the answering machine.

"I just saw the shrine stones going up in your clubhouse fireplace, Mr. Martineau. Have you any idea how unpopular that will make you with Chuparrosa's citizens?"

"Oh, come now, Sanchez," Martineau scoffed. "Who knows anything about those rocks? The Archaeological Club, a few horse people from the county and Agatha Pure Stone. That's all. What other clubhouse in the area has such a unique spiritual feature? They set us apart. I'm just now planning a brochure around them."

"If you put them back where they came from, you could plan a park around them, an amenity, and be thought of as a philanthropist."

"And have Agatha frightening my residents away?" Martineau sighed. "You don't understand this business, Marshal. We can't afford to be patrons of archaeology. It's exclusivity that's sells lots. We have to have perks that no one else offers. You know—something to one-up your friends. The residents of Sonoran Skyline aren't likely to be interested in parks. They'll be playing golf and showing off their clubhouse. The stones'll be protected and well taken care of. Just like in a museum." He chuckled and Sanchez sensed that as far as Sonoran Skyline was concerned, the matter was settled.

"But I've been meaning to call you," Martineau went on. "The new guards are working out well. We had no trouble at all last night. However, Marshal, those picketers are a royal pain. I don't suppose you can get rid of them."

The marshal pointed out that there was that little matter of the right to peaceably assemble.

"Well," Martineau said, "so far they are peaceable, and there aren't many of them. We'll hope they soon get sunburned and quit.

Ambition and ignorance are a dangerous combination, Sanchez thought. He hung up and punched in Lucia's number. She met his announcement of the petroglyph's new home address with shocked silence, then angry sputtering.

"But—but doesn't he know what those are?" she stammered. "Doesn't he appreciate their uniqueness? He can't put a shrine in a fireplace!"

"Oh, Roger understands just how unusual the stones are," Hank assured her. "It's just the spiritual feature he needs in the clubhouse to sell his lots."

More silence. Then Lucia sputtered again. "What if I explained to him that they are much more valuable *in situ* and offered the club's help in establishing and protecting a small park around them?"

"Worth a try, Lucia," Hank said, though he knew it was hopeless. "You might be able to catch him at his office now."

When Deputy Rhys Jones came limping across the outer office, followed by Kevin Dingle, Sanchez waved them in and motioned for them to close the door. It was time to get a couple of ears to the ground in Chuparrosa. The deputies' profiles were a shade lower than his, and they were both locals. After a year as marshal, Hank was still viewed as a foreigner, a Mexican, in the Anglo community. His ethnicity tightened local tongues.

"You can stop searching for the missing petroglyphs," he told them. "They're about to be part of the fireplace at the new Castle Rock Clubhouse."

Kevin blurted out an expletive as he slouched against the doorframe. Jones lowered his stocky frame into a chair opposite the marshal's desk, stretching out his game leg, a reminder of his rodeo days.

"Martineau's got 'em now, huh?" He groaned. "That sure oughta bring out more pickets."

Sanchez nodded. "What do you hear about the water troubles?"

Kevin, fresh off patrol, gave a shrug. "The pickets look miserable. There's not much traffic on Buckskin Trail, so they don't get to demonstrate very often. They say Roger Martineau keeps driving by with his nose in the air."

"Any whispers about the dog's death or why the golf course sprinklers came on in the daytime? The Spanish Saddle Mountain residents I've talked to claim they had nothing to do with those acts. Who else would be interested in shutting down the golf courses?"

Kevin and Rhys glanced at each other. "The ones who've talked to us don't have a clue," the older man said. "But they're cheering. They think ol' Roger's getting' what he deserves."

Sanchez swiveled his chair to watch the tourists on Gold Dust Road. A few people bustled between shops, hurrying through the sunny stretches into the shade of trees and overhangs. The coming influx of snowbirds and winter residents in October would signal a longed-for end to the deep economic trough that was summer. There are too many elements in these troubles that we're missing, he thought. We can't wait much longer to find them.

He tossed his pencil, making it rattle into the Taos pot on his desk and stood up. "Okay guys, keep listening. Keep asking questions," he ordered, clearing his throat in an effort to soften the harshness in his voice. "I want detailed notes of any conversations you have with folks. Record any threats, any attitudes, any rumors, even if you get them at a bar some night. Detailed, understand?"

Things could get a lot rougher. He couldn't shake a sense of something evil stalking the town. He was damn well not going to let anyone get hurt. Especially Pella.

An hour later Clair Tubbs from the Chuparrosa Hummer ducked in at his door, overflowing with her usual assertiveness. Flopping her plump body into the guest chair, she dug a note pad out of her black bag and touched her tongue to the tip of a pencil.

Sanchez winced. He was never glad to see Claire Tubbs. A strange blend of coyness and perseverance, the reporter clamped on every story with her bulldog grip. Her unbridled imagination exceeded her search for the truth, and the inaccuracy of quotes she attributed to him in her articles never failed to embarrass him.

"I've come from interviewing the Martineau's about their dog, Marshal. I'd like a statement from you, too, for our Monday edition.

Mrs. Martineau claimed the dog simply drowned, but there's this rumor going around that someone killed him…" She let the words hang in the air, pencil hovering above her paper, waiting for him to confirm or deny the story.

"How about a cup of coffee, Claire? Cream? Sugar?"

"Black." She gave him a saucy smile and tucked a lock of limp brown hair behind her ear. He was always baffled by her efforts to flirt with him.

Sanchez stepped over to the pot on the cabinet and filled a plastic cup. Given Claire's gift for drama, the tale could go anywhere. He wondered what she knew about the sprinklers, the extra guards at Sonoran Skyline and the threat to Pella. She was a nosy woman, often nosy for the pure hell of it. He was not going to allow his investigation to be tainted by the urban legends she loved to dream up.

He turned to hand her the coffee and saw the smug grin of a woman who believes her suspicions have been confirmed. She took a sip, crossed her well-padded legs and sank back into the chair. It was clear she wasn't leaving until she'd heard the whole tale.

Sanchez perched on the corner of the desk and tried the smile he reserved for beguiling susceptible ladies. With a big, shocking headline, it might be possible to roll those sacred stones right back to the bank of the creek. And Roger Martineau be damned!

"Claire," he began, "I wonder if you've seen the circle of prehistoric petroglyphs along Devil's Eye Creek? You've seen them? And you know Agatha Pure Stone? Good. Then let me give you an exclusive story for your front page. A very controversial story. And I'll even tell you who to interview."

Claire's eyes widened as new opportunities flowered before them. "Oh, Hank!" There was a catch in her voice. She wet her lips in anticipation. "That would be so wonderful. Shoot!"

Chapter 9

There were plenty of parking spaces near the Chuparrosa High School gym when Pella arrived late that afternoon. At 5:30 most of the students and teachers had gone on to other activities. A white van, with the flamboyant logo "Fiesta Flores & Company," painted in salsa colors on both sides, made a gaudy splash among the drab pickups. Maud's sleek burgundy MG was nowhere to be seen.

"That old lady had better turn up," Pella thought as she walked the path toward the building. It hadn't been easy persuading Mr. Bates, the head custodian, to come with the young man who did the light and sound for a confrontation with the pageant's director. He'd dealt with Maude before and wasn't interested in arguing about lighting, as he put it, "with some zany broad." Pella knew she'd have to act as referee. The atmosphere around Maude tended to be charged with emotion.

The cavernous gym was dark, but the stage gleamed with footlights and overhead spots. On the fringes, volunteer stagehands peered out through the wing curtains. She recognized Tyler Bent and Jerry Morley among them.

Spanish music pulsed from a boom box at the back of the stage, and in the center Fiesta Flores and a partner circled each other like fighters, close, but never touching. The man, shoulders forward, menacing arms spread wide, hovered over Fiesta, while she taunted him with her arched body, sometimes advancing, sometimes darting behind him, the deep ruffles on her dress foaming about her stomping feet. Their eyes locked on each other, hot, passionate. The hypnotizing click of her black castanets throbbed like a beating heart.

The stagehands' jaws dropped and the reality of Friday afternoon in the local gym dissolved in the unspoken sensuality of the performance.

As the music rose in crescendo, the pair of dancers continued turning back and forth, sweeping around each other, feet pounding the dusty floor. Two elegant figures, like tightly coiled springs, tempting each other with violence and seduction. By the time the flamenco rhythms faded away, Pella's mouth was open, too, and she clapped and hollered *"¡Ole!* "along with the crew.

Fiesta, her black hair shining in the overhead lights, laughed at the applause and dropped a low curtsy, before turning to consult with her partner.

"¡Magnifico, Fiesta, *mi amor!"* Maude appeared out of the darkness to exchange a few words with the couple on stage. "Are they not gorgeous?" she called to Pella as the pair undulated out of sight between the curtains. "Wait until you hear the guitarist they will have for the performance. It is all a tribute to the Spanish influences in our community. Granted there are not many. I guess architecture is the main one now. Of course, all of us have Mexican gardeners and maids." She heaved a noisy sigh. "So lovely to again work with professionals like Fiesta and her troupe. Now, where is that janitor? I just ducked in here for a minute, my dear. I have to grab a bite and be back here at eight for the children's rehearsal. No great art is created on an empty stomach."

"Superintendent, Maude," Pella hissed and glanced over her shoulder, afraid the man would vanish if he heard himself so maligned. She caught sight of Mr. Bates, attended by a young man in jeans, beneath the basketball hoop and hustled all three of them forcibly up to the stage. Everybody looked edgy. Maude batted her eyes and began pitching every theatre word she could remember at the two men, while Mr. Bates countered with electrical terms. This was not communication.

"Now both of you stop it," Pella ordered. "You're only confusing us. We're here to learn from each other." She held out her hand to the other man. "You're Chris Holmes? Thanks for coming to help get the pageant off to a successful start." She leafed through the pages on her clipboard and passed program schedules to each of them . "Maude, let's go through the acts, and you can tell Mr. Bates and Mr. Holmes exactly what lighting you want for each one of them. I'll make notes and get plenty of copies for you by tomorrow."

"But there are the spots, too," Maud hedged.

"Mr. Holmes, do you live in Chuparrosa?" Pella asked.

Caught off guard, the man nodded, looking suspicious.

"Well, you'd be doing a fantastic service for the town if you worked the spots on Friday and Saturday nights."

"Could I bring my girl friend to help?"

"Absolutely. Free tickets for your whole family. You, too, Mr. Bates. Both nights." Pella steered them over to the electrical panel and began marking down the orders Maude issued, as interpreted by Mr. Bates.

"Now for Fiesta's number we need a clear tight spot on a darkened stage," she proclaimed. "And you have got to follow them around with it. Do not let them dodge off into oblivion."

"You bet we can do that." A wholehearted smile lit Bates' face. "Boy, she is some sexy babe, isn't she?"

Maude drew back in horror. "That is art, Mr. Bates! Exciting, passionate art."

Bates' imagination turned his smile into a leer. "Yeah, it sure is!"

An hour later the list was complete. Chris Holmes, exuding confidence, dashed off to another job, and Pella guided Maude to her car, while Mr. Bates stayed behind in the empty gym to shut off the lights and shoo out the last of the stagehands. Only four vehicles remained in the parking lot. The sun had dipped below the western edge of Chisos Mesa half an hour before and low walking lights formed isolated yellow rings on the blacktopped walkway.

"Well, that is one thing off my mind." Maude held Pella's arm as they groped their way across the gravel parking lot in the deepening dusk. "That is a nice looking boy you brought in to do the lights, Pella. Not like Mr. Bates. It is such a good thing I can get along with all kinds of people. God knows I have had lots of practice. My dear George knew nothing about the theatre, either, but my ability to communicate my needs saved our marriage many times."

Clipboard under her arm, Pella helped Maude drape herself over the leather seat of her car and tucked in all her bits of clothing before slamming the door. "I'll type our notes tomorrow and e-mail copies to you all. Who else should get one?"

Maude snapped on her headlights and the MG roared. "Blast! It is nearly seven," she wailed as the dashboard lit up. "I must fly!"

Pella jumped back to keep her toes from being flattened as the car sped off. "I'll make twenty copies," she thought as she walked to her Honda through the settling dust, fumbling in her purse for keys. "Maude will lose at least nineteen."

It was a cloudless night. A thumbnail moon glowed, the brightest light in a royal blue sky. High up a pair of nighthawks practiced their aerobatics in silhouette. No monsoon clouds puffed up in the east, and the light wind from the south felt dry and caressing. Signs of fall, Pella wondered? It was the start of her second year in Chuparrosa. The ill omens of the past were fading and the town was beginning to feel familiar, like a home. She had an identity here now, a job and friends. And Hank. A rare sense of good fortune wrapped her in its sudden warmth.

The passing breeze blew the man's scent across Pella's nostrils an instant before she felt his hand tighten over her mouth. Another strong hand slipped the heavy bag off her shoulder, twisting the straps painfully about her wrists, its weight locking them tight. He smelled of animals, clean and earthy at the same time. She squirmed and felt the prick of a knife on her neck, as he pried the car keys out of her rigid fingers.

"Scream, and you get it here and now, babe." There was an obscene gaiety in the husky mutter. Intense with pleasure. She recognized the throbbing voice on her answering machine and fought the straps that bound her hands. The knife dug deeper.

"I'm a bare inch away from your jugular, babe." He chuckled. "Such a pretty, pale neck. I'd like to keep you alive so we can have that swim. And don't you go worrying about a swim suit."

The knife's pressure faltered for an instant while he reached for the car door. She heard the distant clip of footsteps on the walk from the gym. Somebody coming, taking long strides, heading for his car. Brisk and purposeful. The man had heard them, too. He let go of the door handle, his arm squeezing her like a python, the point of the blade biting once more, this time deeper.

"Quiet as the grave, luv." His breath blew hot on her face.

She dropped her chin and stretched down, reaching for the bulky lavaliere. Her shoulders rose as she fought for another quarter inch, bobbing her head to hit the mark, feeling the knife slicing into her jaw, the ooze of blood tickling her neck. He began dragging her away from the footsteps, into the shadows at the back of the Honda.

"One more wiggle, and you bleed to death here and now." It was a command. The voice had gone frigid.

Again she missed the mark, but this time she picked up both feet and went limp against him. He stumbled, the sudden burden pulling him off balance. The car keys clattered on the ground. The knife turned and sliced down, as he fought to keep his grip on her. A glancing blow with her chin on the lavaliere and the thing shrieked, screamed at last, just before she hit the pavement and scooted away from him to the shelter of the car.

The awful sound circled her head, terrible in its shrillness, blocking out all other noise. She flopped on her stomach, unweaving her hands from the straps, ready to bob to her knees, and dash into the darkness. An outstretched arm halted her escape.

"What in hell is goin' on? Turn that damn thing off, will you?" Tyler Bent held his free hand over one ear, his eyes squinting in reaction to the siren's howl.

Pella fumbled with the device, searching for a switch. "Where'd he go?" she screamed over the noise.

Tyler glanced around. "Vanished, I guess. Here, let me do that." He grabbed for the chain. "You'll have the whole neighborhood out here. Why is it wet? Can't you take it off?"

Her shaking hands could not undo the clasp. Cursing, Bent broke the chain and ground the alarm under his heel, as a pickup skidded into the parking lot, yellow lights flashing. A man in jeans jumped out and came running.

"Get away from her!" he shouted, pistol pointed at Bent. "You in trouble, lady? Shit, you're bleedin'."

Pella leaned against the car, eyes closed, teeth chattering. "Th-there was a man. He had a knife," she gasped. "I don't know where he went." She put her hand to her throat, feeling the sticky mess there and on her shirt.

"I'm the night security here." The man surveyed Bent with suspicion. "Come sit in my truck while I call 911."

Pella ducked to the ground for her purse and keys. "Not for me. I'm going home." She took a sobbing breath and stumbled against Bent, who held on to her as she gave in to tears. "But I-I – have to find my clipboard."

"Lady, you're bleedin'. You might faint or somethin'." The man's frown begged her to be reasonable.

Tyler dug a bandanna handkerchief out of his pocket and pushed it into her hand. "First aid," he explained. "I'll drive the lady home."

"But I gotta make a report for my boss and the marshal," the guard persisted. "The marshal will wanna investigate."

"The marshal'll be waiting on my doorstep." She tried to stop crying, clenching her teeth to keep them quiet. "He'll be dancing a jig because he was right."

Tyler put a hand under her elbow and steered her to the passenger side of the Honda. "My name's Tyler Bent," he called over his shoulder. "With the Forest Service. This is Pella VanDoren. She works at the city hall and sleeps with the marshal. I'll drive her home right now."

Caught off guard, the man wavered, but didn't try to stop them. Bent jumped in beside Pella and lifted the keys from her hand. The car roared to life, and they bounced down to the main road, Pella shuddering uncontrollably, the bandanna pressed to her jaw.

"You jerk," she sputtered. "I don't sleep with the marshal."

"Hell, it got you away from Mr. Security." He was laughing at her. "Don't you really? If I'm not cuttin' in on the marshal's territory, maybe you'll go out with me again."

"I'm not anybody's territory!" she yelled, her frenzy mounting. "We're friends, just very good friends." Pella lay back against the headrest, moving her jaw to see if it still worked. "Did my clipboard get in? I've got to have my clipboard."

"Back seat." Bent swung the car onto her street. "Who grabbed you, Pella? Was he going to rape you?"

She swallowed to keep from sobbing. "I don't know. He came up in back of me. You must have seen him."

"Only a silhouette, all black. Then he was gone, and I was trying to stop the noise."

"It was nothing! Nothing!" The shudders were beginning again. She couldn't talk about it.

The car lights, as they turned into Pella's driveway, illuminated the figure of Marshal Sanchez pacing back and forth on her front walk. He was scowling like a bandit.

"Nothin', huh?" Tyler turned toward her, one eyebrow raised. "Swell. So go tell that to your very good friend."

Chapter 10

Sanchez banged the cell phone down on the bedside table and swung himself into motion, fumbling in his closet for a clean shirt.

It had been a short night, most of it spent in his office in case an alarm came through the switchboard from Pella's apartment. Now, at dawn, after a couple hours of sleep, he'd gotten a call from his third deputy, Gus Kremer.

"Sorry to bother you at home, Marshal," Gus had said. The words had a strangled sound. Sanchez could hear angry, incoherent screams from Roger Martineau in the background. "We've got a new problem over here at Sonoran Skyline."

"What's going on?"

He'd heard Gus take a deep breath to begin the explanation, when the phone was suddenly wrenched away, and Martineau's voice shrilled, "Sanchez, get your butt over here!" Then the phone was slammed down.

Fifteen minutes later, Hank and Gus stood beside what had been one of the most pristine golf greens in the country. Now the smooth velvet of emerald bent grass was pockmarked with deep u-shaped prints, the turf torn into ragged patches, exposing dirt and sand.

Off to the side of the rolling fairway, in the taller grass, lay one of the control panels used by the maintenance people to manually adjust irrigation to the greens. It had been pulled over, the pedestal broken off at the ground, the panel smashed. Wires of different colors splayed in all directions.

Roger Martineau couldn't stand still. He hopped about the perimeter of the green in a crazy dance. "See what they've done!" His voice rose to a squeaky pitch as he raged. "They've destroyed a multimillion dollar enterprise over a little water." Shouting curses at the cloudless blue sky, he ran down the slope to caress the control panel and fondle the wires lying broken in the rough.

Sanchez frowned at the ruined turf. Horses had been ridden over the green again and again at a gallop until the grass was kicked up in ridges. It looked as if the control panel had been lassoed and toppled to the ground by someone on horseback. Hoof prints led into the desert scrub beyond.

"How many others?"

"The fourth and eighth on Castle Rock," Roger wheezed, "sixth and first on Mogollon, the twelfth and this one on Ocotillo. The control panels on each one." He snatched off his aviator sunglasses to wipe the back of a hand across his eyes. "Those had just been sodded and watered. They knew exactly what they were going for!"

"We'll bring in the county sheriff's people," Hank said. He didn't want to, but there wasn't any choice now. Most of the damage was on county land, outside Chuparrosa city limits.

Sanchez understood all too well the need for water in this arid country. Without it the foothills would be one dusty ghost town, unfit for human habitation. Many Chuparrosans had the gut feeling that too much of the Sonoran Desert was being scraped clean, replaced by houses and golf courses, while the special places they valued were destroyed. This small, factional dispute had finally exploded, splattering its dirt in all directions. He didn't want to admit to the county police that somebody in his town could be so destructive.

The attack on Pella the night before had been a nightmare. He'd taken her to the clinic to be patched up and stayed, holding her until the shudders stopped. When her roommate, Glory Windom, came home, he'd refused to leave their apartment unless they promised to sleep with the security alarm engaged. It had been a noisy argument. He'd finally won.

Pella hadn't fallen apart, *gracias, Senor.* With a forced self-control, he'd managed to keep from yelling at her for running off to the high school without telling him. The effort to stay calm had exhausted them both. Well, he'd made too many mistakes with this guy. He couldn't afford any more.

Hank glanced at his watch. A quarter to seven. Pella would be getting up soon. The minute she opened her door she was in danger. He'd planned to follow her around all day, but he couldn't justify that now. Rhys Jones would have to take some extra duty.

"How many horses?" he asked Gus.

His deputy squinted and scratched his head. "Two, I'd say."

The marshal nodded in agreement. "What did your patrol see, Mr. Martineau?"

"Nothing!" the older man yelped. "They drove around here all night with their eyes closed. They're probably in cahoots with this maniac. Some great idea that was, bringing in those idiots. You ought to get the bill for their time." He clenched a fist and punched it at the green. "And for this!"

"Tu madre, hombre!" Sanchez thought with fresh bitterness. "We'll talk in your office, Mr. Martineau. I'll call the county sheriff's office and my deputy from there. Don't let your people touch anything!"

Two hours later, Sanchez was planting his boots with care across the farthest fairway. For most of that time, he'd been following hoof prints made by the horses as they'd moved from green to green. There had been two horses, two riders, sometimes walking side-by-side, sometimes nose-to-tail.

A couple of delinquents out for an evening's joy ride would have cantered down the open fairways, but this pair sneaked in and out, running the horses only when they were methodically messing up the greens they'd chosen to destroy. Those six, Martineau squealed over and over in anguish, had been recently re-sodded, so the roots hadn't yet taken deep hold on the soil beneath. Somehow the riders had known which greens were the most vulnerable, and they'd ridden them just after the late night watering.

What *bobo* on the Spanish Saddle Mountain water committee would risk jail time and a huge fine to make a point? For Roger, uprooting the pre-historic shrine had been a clever business decision, but destroying his shrine to golf was a desecration, and he'd make the guilty parties pay plenty. It meant that Chuparrosa citizens would have to choose up sides again.

Martineau had brushed aside the attack on Pella the night before and demanded that she come to open the office in this emergency. Sanchez figured she'd be safe enough there with all the sheriff's deputies around. A quick phone call to Rhys Jones had covered her home-to-office travel. Then he'd sipped a cup of coffee and tried to keep his temper while he waited for the team of county deputies to arrive. In the background, *el jeffe* Martineau paced, alternately moaning or shrieking epithets aimed at him and his deputies.

County police were at that moment scouring the damaged areas for any clue. They'd found one decent footprint in a damp bunker before Hank left to follow the whole trail. A dainty cowboy boot, from the look of it – a narrow instep and high heel, about size four. Not a man's shoe. A second set of prints had a much larger foot and a much worn flat heel, but was too messed up to get a clear cast.

On the seat of an overturned stone bench, one officer had spotted a baffling bit of graffiti that Roger claimed was fresh. "Is 411718" it said. At least, that was as close as anyone could come to reading it. The county guys shook their bewildered heads and photographed it from all angles. No one made any guesses about what it meant.

Hank yanked off his broad brimmed hat to wipe his forehead. It was close to nine o'clock. The morning breeze, quickened by the rising temperature, blew in small bursts, drying the back of his shirt. The temperature had been 100 degrees the day before, and it was expected to match that today, with humidity in the single digits. He settled his hat on his head again, the brim low so he could look east toward the folded slopes of Spanish Saddle Mountain. All those people had horses. The entire mountain was zoned for horse set-ups. Fiesta might have a small, elegant foot like the print. She'd love this kind of lark, but would she risk her reputation for a cause? He didn't think so. She was too smart. Too selfish.

Moving on to the higher elevation, Sanchez left the shallow, bowl-shaped valley that held Sonoran Skyline. The National Forest lay ahead of him to the north. Far to the south the highway spun its switch-backed way between the foothills to Phoenix. He'd left the irrigated fairways, the palm trees, and the foreign smell of living grass behind. The change of vegetation was sudden and dramatic. Out in the waterless sand, burrsage leaves crackled as he brushed against them, and the leafless branches of ocotillo reached for the sky. To the uninitiated the desert looked dead, but he'd lived in deserts long enough to understand that this dry vegetation was clever. It was only sleeping. The occasional quarter inch of rain could keep it alive; an inch would turn it green and make it blossom.

A shrubby cat claw acacia grabbed at his damp shirt, and he stopped to unhook the curved spines while he studied ground once more. The hoof prints were harder to follow in the granite chips covering the desert floor. Stepping with care to avoid obliterating the trail, he reached the barbed wire fence that marked the forest boundary. The strands of wire had been cut between fence posts and looped aside to make an entrance for the riders. Caught on the barbs, coarse black hairs from a horse's tail floated in the breeze. Sanchez pulled a collection bag from his pocket and sealed them inside.

Beyond the fence rose a hill of granite sand that spread into a larger ridge. A rock squirrel fled before him and lizards scuttled to the shady sides of boulders. There were four sets of clear tracks on the lower sandy edge of the hill. The riders had ridden back the way they'd come.

When he reached the place where the hill curved to the north, he could see the forest road: number 587, rarely graded, impassable after a rain, requiring caution at any time. With no trails to the golf course or north into the forest wilderness from 587, the road got little traffic. Agatha Pure Stone lived a mile farther on at the road's dead end.

Kevin Dingle, his patrol car parked in the shade of a palo verde, just off number 587, raised his arm and grinned. "It's right where you said it'd be, Marshal," the deputy called. As Sanchez got closer, Kevin pointed to the dusty road between them. "Double horse trailer, I'd say, and a truck of some kind pullin' it."

Hank skidded down the final bank onto the road and studied the ground. In the four days since the rain, the dust had dried and now lay soft and silky, ready to be rearranged by every passing wind. Kevin's reading of the impressions on the road might be accurate, but it was tough to tell for sure. Horses had been here. Fresh droppings lay in the weeds. The tracks went no farther.

"Bald tires?"

Dingle nodded. "Yeah. There's a fair footprint over here, though."

Off to the side was another impression of the slim cowboy boot, the exaggerated point of the toe pressed in firmly where its owner had pushed up into the saddle from the spongy soil under the mesquite tree. Only a trace of the half-circle heel was visible. Could it have been a child, Hank wondered? But who'd involve a child in an adventure like this?

"Want me to take a cast of that one?" Dingle circled the print cautiously. "Then we can go lookin' for Cinderella."

They photographed the site, then collected and noted what trash littered the ditches, a gift for the County Sheriff's lab. While Kevin cast the footprint, the marshal hiked half a mile to the Buckskin Trail blacktop that led to Chuparrosa and strung a "don't cross" streamer between a mesquite tree on one side and a creosote bush on the other. The sheriff's people would want to see the site. Indistinct prints of the truck and trailer continued to the main road. There they disappeared. It was impossible to tell which way the truck and trailer had gone after they pulled onto the dust-worn blacktop.

When the marshal returned, Kevin was clucking with delight over his cast of the footprint. "Follow this road to where it fords Devil's Eye Creek," Hank said to his deputy as they loaded their equipment. "Let's ask Agatha if she saw anything last night."

The track deteriorated even more as they headed west, followed by a trail of beige dust spiraling in the air. Kevin drove slowly, avoiding the deepest ruts, and crossed the ford by maneuvering between the white, lime-crusted boulders that had given the creek its name. On the far bank, the trail turned south, out of the National Forest, ending at the short lane to Agatha's hut and garden.

The woman's head could be seen over the top of the irrigation ditch that ran from the creek. She straightened and pushed her hair out of her eyes when she heard the car drive up. As the men got out, she climbed the bank and came toward them, hollering her version of a Hohokam greeting.

"Wacko old lady," Kevin muttered.

They met at the corner of her garden, a plot of bushy plants, ringed by a fence of ocotillo sticks. She looked more disheveled than usual, arms, legs and muslin gown muddy from the creek, clumps of gray hair plastered on her damp face. She beamed at them with pleasure and repeated the welcome.

"What are you growing, Agatha?" Hank asked, easing into the conversation.

"Tepary beans, tomatillos, peppers. They don't take much water. Lucky, too, because the creek is getting lower than it's ever been. The bugs leave 'em alone." Her weathered face wrinkled as she smiled, brown eyes innocent as a child's. "I've got beans cookin', if you'd care to have some." She nodded at the adobe oven sagging against her hut.

The thin streak of smoke, drifting toward the east from its chimney, smelled of chilis and tomatillos. It reminded Hank that he'd missed breakfast.

She passed out bowls of steaming beans, motioned them into the shade of a palo verde tree, while she plopped cross-legged on the ground with a groan, one hand rubbing her back. The men hunkered down on their heels. Kevin eyed the beans with suspicion, while Sanchez tucked into them, savoring the burn of chilis, the aroma of cilantro. He cleaned the bowl, aware that she watched him, gratified by the signs of his pleasure.

"Mighty fine beans, Agatha," he began. It was time to get down to the questions. "Your neighbors had some trouble last night. Do you know anything about that?"

"Sonoran Skyline has strung its own loom and woven its own fate," she said at last, frowning. "They stole the shrine stones to use in their fireplace. It was a wicked and irreverent act."

"Tell me what you saw or heard last night. Anything unusual?"

She stared at them, bitterness clouding her face. "It was an act of war, but it had to be done. The animals will die without the shrine stones. How are you to get them back?"

"I thought Bent explained that to you," Hank said. Of course she wouldn't understand. Even he didn't understand. "The petroglyphs belong to Sonoran Skyline. Some bureaucratic bungling none of us has any control over. But the stones haven't gone far, Agatha. The animals should be all right."

The woman's eyes drooped, and she began to rock back and forth in a hypnotic rhythm. "My neighbors will have more trouble. We all will. But theirs will be the worst."

"Hell, you can't get those stones back to their site, anyway," Kevin burst out, his voice impatient. "They're cemented in that damn wall."

The rocking continued. Her face was closed now, a peaceful smile flickering over it. "Oh, the stones will come back to their places. After the troubles. Terrible things will happen. I've seen them in the smoke. But afterwards the shrine will be replaced. I've been assured by the mysteries." She began to hum in a low monotone.

"What terrible things, Agatha?" Hank asked, trying to draw her out of the trance.

She refused to come. Her lips moved, repeating the mumbled words she had invented to describe her world. Exchanging glances, the men stood up and walked back through the heat to their patrol car.

"Old witch! Bet she's put a curse on all of us." Kevin kicked a rock with his boot, sending it spinning over the bank. They heard the ominous plop as it dropped, a dead weight, into the shadowed waters of Devil's Eye Creek.

Chapter 11

Tyler Bent, his long, untidy frame sprawled in a chair across the desk from the marshal, asked the question that had been bothering Hank. "Now that half the town is at war with Sonoran Skyline, who's going to tell you which law-abiding citizen tore up the golf greens?"

"We'll find out," Hank growled, with a show of confidence he didn't feel. "We can sure as hell rule out the golfers."

The marshal's just completed session with the mayor had not brightened his weekend. The damaged golf course had made Mel Bergen almost as furious as Roger Martineau. During an interview at his home, Bergen, jaw clenched, face purple, had demanded that Hank provide him with detailed reports of that destruction and the attack on Pella. He wanted them on his desk by noon today. The marshal had no time to waste gossiping about it with Bent.

"I saw Agatha yesterday." Tyler scratched fingers through his beard, bleached blond from hours in the sun, and curled forward off his spine. The gold stud in his earlobe winked as it caught the light. "How does she think she'll get the stones back? She said someone would be helping her."

"But she didn't say who."

Bent shook his head, peeled his body from the chair and stood up to reach for a sun Katchina on the bookcase. "Nice one." He turned it over and squinted to examine the signature. "You know the guy who made this?"

"Yeah. Did Agatha give you any idea what kind of connection she'd made? The Water Committee, the Archaeology Club, ancient Hohokam spirits?"

The other man fluffed the Kachina's feathers and put it back on the shelf. "Nope, but I'd go with the Hohokam spirits. She's still warning that the animals will die, and she's predicting dire consequences for Sonoran Skyline." A grin flickered over his face. "I guess ol' Roger thinks that closing his courses on a weekend is about as dire as it gets."

"Right." Sanchez snapped. Roger, shaking his fist at the sky this morning, had sworn vengeance on his Spanish Saddle Mountain neighbors with all the fervor of an Old Testament prophet. Then, scrounging for a handier scapegoat, he'd settled the blame for his troubles on the marshal's office. He'd been trembling with fury as Hank walked away from him to track the hoof prints over greens and on to the forest road. "Damn stupid Mexican," the man had mumbled loud enough for everyone to hear. It brought frowns to the faces of the county officers Hank had been briefing,

When the marshal rode back with Kevin to collect his pickup, he'd found Pella, groggy and pale, at her desk in the sales office. Six or seven wild-eyed real estate people surrounded her, arguing about what to tell their clients to minimize the psychic damage. She'd deftly brushed aside all comments on the over-sized Band-Aids that covered her wounds.

"Cut myself shaving," she quipped to a couple of young realtors, who had pushed through the crowd to demand instant attention. The phone was pressed between her ear and shoulder, while she dug in a drawer for more maps of the courses, and scribbled in red across the greens that were being repaired.

The new lavaliere hung around her neck, *gracias a Dios.* Sanchez knew he'd have to count on the confusion in the office to keep her attacker from trying again. After he'd arranged to pick her up for lunch, he'd driven off for the unpleasant session with the mayor.

"Umm...How's Pella doing?" Bent asked.

The question sounded innocent, but Sanchez raised his head. Is that what you're here to talk about? Hands off, *cabron.*

"I took her to the ER for some patching up last night. A few stitches along her jaw."

"And stayed the night?"

Hank shook his head. God knows he'd tried to argue for a bed on her sofa, but Pella wasn't buying it. "Her roommate came home. They promised to sleep with the alarm on." And he'd spent most of an uncomfortable night stretched between two chairs in his office in case an alarm from her apartment came through the switchboard. "This morning she's hard at work at the sales office."

Bent looked impressed. "She's all right then?"

"She's getting along fine without either of us." Sanchez tried to keep the regret out of his voice. In a sense he was proud of her courage. Luisa, his ex-wife, had avoided most problems by giving in to varying degrees of hysteria. He'd gotten used to shielding her from the knocks of life, in part to protect himself from the scenes. But his work as an Albuquerque cop had been unpredictable and dangerous. When he'd come home bloodied by a stray bullet that had just missed his eye, Luisa had packed her bags and gone to live with her parents in the mountains of northern New Mexico. Now she had a sheepherder husband and a couple of toddlers.

Hank shuffled the papers scattered on his desk. "Will you get out of here? I've got reports to write."

"One more thing before I go." Bent shuffled his feet. "I caught a rumor circulating in the Forest Service Office this morning. I thought I'd go down now to check it out." He paused, measuring Hank's attention. "Seems there's a gauge to measure the water level on Devil's Eye Creek about a mile south of St. Jude's Peak. They tell me, for the first time since it's been keeping records, there's nothing to measure."

"It's dry?" Sanchez felt anger bubble up in his throat. "It's dry!" What was it Agatha had said about the stretch of creek on her property?

"As dust. 'Course we're in a drought. Just a few drops of rain since March. But the Creek's touted as a free-flowing stream. Hundreds of species of wildlife, flocks of migrating birds. And, best of all, tourists who come to see them."

"That's state land, isn't it?" Hank tried to calm his mind, searching for an angle he could use. "Why's the Forest Service interested?"

"Every creek depends on the underground water tables. When the aquifer is up, the excess flows to the creeks. When it falls below a certain point, the water from the creeks flow back into it. We've had no rain to fill them up, so eventually we'll see riparian vegetation dying. Very bad for everybody's business."

"And they think it's three years of Sonoran Skyline's pumping for their golf courses that's created this?"

"Combined with their fifty new homes, the wells, the drought and all the 115 degree days we had this past summer. It's sucked down the aquifer so far that the creek's drying up."

"But the reservoirs still have water."

"Good snowmelt from former years keeps the water flowing through the pipes. It's different with wells. The aquifer isn't as easily replenished."

"What about state sanctions? County?"

"Goals, but no sanctions. Nothing they can threaten people with. Sonoran Skyline has a grandfathered right to use the aquifer." Bent shook his head. "Strange how we've always been in denial about water around this state. As long as there's a glass of $H2O$ in the pipe and stacks of little bottles at the grocery store, why worry?"

He moved to the door. "Anyway, I'm going to drive down and have a look for myself. I'll let you know what I find." He grinned. "Then I guess I'll drop over to the Skyline sales office and tell Pella I'll be glad to come to her rescue anytime."

Pella called before noon to let Sanchez know she'd be working all day.

"We're on the run over here. The place is still a mad house. Roger's dealing with the county cops and rescheduling the golfers, while I reassure the realtors and the residents."

"Dinner, then."

She hesitated. "I'm going to be exhausted."

"I'll pick you up at the sales office at five. Don't move until I get there." It would still be light out at that time of the afternoon. With plenty of people around, she should be safe. "We'll get carryout on the way to your place, if you like."

Another hesitation. "I thought an evening by myself might be nice. A bubble bath, early to bed."

"Not as long as you're being stalked." His tone sounded dogmatic even to himself. He knew from experience that wasn't the way to persuade her, so he changed his tactics. "The bath and bed are okay, but don't count on being alone until this creep is caught."

"You mean I'm bait?"

He grasped at the idea. She'd refuse his protection, but give him her help. "That's it." He heard the beep of call-waiting in the background.

"Hang on," Pella said. A moment later she was back. "Roger. He's working on a coronary. I have to go."

"I'll see you at five. Don't leave the building until I get there," he repeated, but she'd rung off.

"Call me only if it's urgent," Sanchez told dispatcher Linda Smallseed, as he left the report to be faxed to the mayor. He'd checked on the County Sheriff's team and Deputy Kremer out at Sonoran Skyline by cell phone. They'd be finishing up their work later in the afternoon, when he could expect their evaluation. Kevin Dingle was on patrol until four when Rhys took over, then Hank would relieve Gus at Sonoran Skyline. In the meantime, he could be on the spot anywhere in Chuparrosa in a matter of minutes in case of an emergency. So far the vandalism had all happened at night. They could probably relax for a few hours.

He walked west on Gold Dust Road, picking his way through the crowd lining the brick sidewalk to watch the gun battle that Charlie Talaferro staged three times every day of the year, except Christmas. While it couldn't draw the crowd in September that it did in January, there was a respectable number of eager folks waiting for the show to begin. The fact that the performance and outcome were always the same, never seemed to dull the anticipation. When the old west came alive in front of the Miner's Delight Saloon, the crowd cheered its approval.

Sanchez jogged up the steps to the veranda, blinking as he pushed through the swinging doors into the beery dimness of the saloon. Local customers, legs in jeans, feet in boots, leaned their elbows on the shining mesquite wood bar. Jeremiah Morley, his sleeves rolled up, was drawing beers and coasting them to his patrons on the glistening surface with new-found flair. His eyes narrowed when Hank nodded to him, and he began flicking popcorn onto the floor with a bar cloth, as if he were swatting flies.

On the other side of the saloon were booths holding adults and children in shorts, tee shirts and sneakers. They were all shouting to each other over the country music booming in a steady rhythm from the jute box. Waiters wove between the tables, delivering platters of food, while overhead fans rearranged the warm air. The place smelled of malt and browning beef.

Charlie's huge hand clapped Sanchez on the shoulder. "You here for lunch, Marshal?" The owner of the Miner's Delight towered over Hank by a good two inches. His shaggy hair spilled into his eyes and a drooping mustache followed the grooves along his mouth. His angular face had a raffish look, perpetuating the bad-guy image that pumped dollars into his saloon. Hank knew him for a soft touch. "At the bar or a booth?"

"Got time to join me, Charlie?"

A grin spread across Talaferro's face. He led Sanchez to the farthest booth and gave one of his waiters the high sign. "Our special burger all right? On the house." He chuckled. "I gotta keep on the good side of the law."

They settled themselves on opposite sides of the plank table. "I heard about the mess out at Sonoran Skyline," Charlie said. "Don't think much of that."

"Did you hear about Pella?" Alarm flashed in the big man's eyes as Hank filled him in on the attack in the high school parking lot.

"What was on his mind? Rape?"

"Assault of some kind. The guy'd threatened her with drowning."

"Trying to force you to get that water turned off?"

A waiter appeared with plates of burgers, beans and fries, presented with a flourish as he grinned at his boss. Charlie stretched out his hand for the catsup. Steam rising from the beans warmed Hank's face. They didn't smell as tempting as Agatha's.

"It was dark. Bent didn't get a look at him. Pella swears he was the man who left a message on her phone Thursday night. No one she knew. She sensed he was slim and strong, under six feet tall. You see a lot of people, Charlie. Is there anyone of that description hanging around town? Maybe a stranger?"

Charlie passed Hank the catsup, put his elbows on the table and clamped his jaws onto the burger. He chewed, his mustache moving in a steady rhythm, swallowed and took a swig of Coke. "Why would a stranger get himself involved in our water squabble? Why would it matter so much to him that he might be willing to murder a woman?"

The marshal shook his head and began to eat, conscious that the excellent Miner's Delight Special today tasted like sponge. "All right, who do you know in town who's slim and strong and mad at Sonoran Skyline?"

"Slim? That let's out the Morley boys. Old Bud Brickson might be slim, but not strong. Pella'd have no trouble escaping from him. You're sure it's a man?"

Hank shrugged. "We have only Pella's word for it. But she knows all the people you mentioned. And the one you haven't mentioned. Sugar Morley."

Talaferro stirred the puddle of catsup on his plate into concentric circles with a French fry. "Guess you know the Morleys have a redneck vendetta against you. Jerry spouts off occasionally when he thinks I'm out of earshot. They didn't want their land annexed into Chuparrosa three years ago. Now they think they're not getting the attention they should have from the town. They don't like the mayor, either, but at least he's...uh...uh."

"Anglo." The word was as hot as a habanera pepper. It sat on his tongue, burning.

"Yeah," Charlie muttered, looking dangerous. He mashed the French fry into a red pellet on his plate. "Why didn't you lock Pella up after she got that phone call? What are you doin' to protect your woman?"

By her own fierce declaration, Pella wasn't his woman. The delicate balance in their friendship had been established on her terms. All he could do was keep from driving her away and hope for better times in the future.

"I'm trying to keep an eye on her without embarrassing either one of us," he said, jaw clenched. "Damn it, I've got the rest of the town to protect, too."

"'I could not love you half as much, loved I not honor more,'" Charlie quoted and then dropped his head, his face turning the color of the catsup. "Uh...Don't know where that popped from. Martineau and the mayor feel Sonoran Skyline is a higher priority than a life, I take it."

"A multi-million dollar investment usually is."

"Selfish sons-of-bitches." Charlie signaled the waiter to remove the plates and leaned forward on the table. "I'll help you check on her, Hank, and keep my ears open. If I hear or see anything, I'll give you a call." He looked down at the elaborate turquoise and silver watchband on his left wrist, rubbing a finger over the stones. "This rumbling volcano's gonna erupt any day now, Marshal. Where we gonna be when it does?"

Chapter 12

Monday brought a cheap, badly varnished veneer of normalcy to Chuparrosa. There were a few benefits. The mayor had stopped bellowing like an angry buffalo, and two quiet nights had blessed Sanchez with more sleep. He'd even managed some hours off on Sunday.

But alarm bells arrived at dawn on Monday morning, with the copy of The Chuparrosa Hummer that Hank plucked out of the bushes near his doorstep. Claire Tubbs had done her work well, interviewing all the people whose names appeared on the list Hank had given her. Two-inch headlines rose on the front page, leading to stories about the shrine stones' new home, a photographic visit to the site of their installation and an in-the-desert interview with Agatha Pure Stone. The letters-to-the-editor column featured caustic comments by members of the Archaeology Club.

Then the news print gods had blessed her with an even better story: the vandalism on the golf courses, plus a full layout of her photos embellishing page four. When a paper in Phoenix picked up her story, with her by-line, she was transported to reporters' heaven.

So his little scheme hadn't succeeded as planned. He'd bought a bit of time and kept her busy, out of his way. Roger hadn't come out well in the story about the shrine stones. Sensing a smear, he had refused to be interviewed, always a wrong choice for a businessman. Hank was curious to know how the residents at the development would react to all this front page information.

Out at Sonoran Skyline, an expanded maintenance crew, slaving under the lash of Roger Martineau's angry tongue, had restored all three golf courses to playable conditions. Brown patches of mud marred fairways here and there, but the greens had all been re-sodded, the pedestals with their control boxes replaced upright on their bright blankets of bent grass.

The marshal had taken a tour of inspection just before dark on Sunday evening, but he hadn't seen Martineau. Joe Phelps, on duty at the gate, informed him that everybody had headed over to the clubhouse where Greenwood Development was hosting a fancy cocktail party for the residents and lot owners.

"Trying to shore up confidence in the enterprise, so they told me," Joe said, leaning into the window of Hank's pickup, his usual gap-toothed grin replaced by sober lines of concern. "The residents have been pretty rightly spooked by what's been happenin'. Hope they don't think it's my fault." He shook his head, stepping back as Hank eased up on the brake and began to move on. "I sure don't let anybody in unless they're on my list."

There were twice as many pickets across Buckskin trail on Monday morning, when Sanchez drove through the Development gates on his way to the sales office. Most of the new additions, he noticed, were the amateur archaeologists. No discouragement there. Claire Tubbs' articles in the Hummer must have given them a fresh surge of fighting spirit. Sugar Morley stood with her back to the road, waving her hands at the folks gathered around her. A pep talk to the troops, he decided. In spite of the heat, they all grabbed their signs when they saw his car and jiggled them with enthusiasm. There were clever new posters today. Once again he wondered about Sugar's artistic talent.

He'd hoped for an early interview with Martineau when he arrived at the Sonoran Skyline offices, but Pella sat alone in the vast space, her fingers flying over the computer keys. A smaller Band-Aid, taped in the middle of a yellow-purple bruise, covered the stitches on her jaw. She raised her chin and gave him a smile that made her eyes shine.

Sanchez planted his hands on her desk and leaned across to kiss the tip of her nose. "You're sunburned."

"Just there." She patted it with one finger. "How do you think I'd look in the shade of a big cowboy hat like yours?"

"*¡Buenisimo!*" He remembered the way she'd looked the day before at Bartlett Lake, stretched out in the lacy shade of a palo verde tree on a scrap of sandy cove they'd claimed for their own. She'd been wearing nothing but a two-piece suit of spandex, the color of the sky. While she'd watched the sailboats and the water-skiers and pointed out animal shapes in the fat clouds, he'd watched her, seeing the tension uncoil in her body until she was free and relaxed again.

"Oh, get me a spoon with a long handle," she'd murmured at last, looking to the east, where the clouds were piling up above the mountains. "Those mounds are really huge marshmallow sundaes."

"My grandmother called cumulus clouds *la escalera de la ángeles,*" he said, smiling. "Keep watching, because I think the angels are about to come up through the top."

They swam, long easy strokes far out into the lake and back. She swam better than he did, without effort, without getting tired. Halfway back, she sprinted toward the shore and was seated on the blanket toweling her hair when he dropped beside her panting.

"I joined the swim team in high school." Pella tilted her head at him from under the towel and grinned. It was clear that knowing she could beat him if she wished delighted her.

She talked of her dreams of a new job, as she lay staring up through the quivering leaves of the palo verde, a distant smile on her face. It would be something different, exciting and creative. She'd work with enjoyable people, as part of a team, and maybe there'd be a bit of traveling, too, for spice.

"Are you tired of Chuparrosa?" Hank had asked. What if this perfect job turned out to be in California? "Too small for you?" When she swung her puzzled face toward him, he knew belatedly that he'd burst her bubble and scrambled to make amends. "I mean you have friends there. You've become part of the community."

Pella sat up and began to giggle. "Hank, what do you mean? Oh, I know how much they adore me in Chuparrosa." The giggles were becoming convulsive. "Six months ago, I was tossed down a mountain and last week I was knifed. Hank, two people have tried to kill me!" She doubled over, gasping with laughter and sobs.

He caught her in his arms. "*Nena, nena, nena,* You're safe with me! I swear only good things will happen to you from now on." What do I do to the women in my life, he wondered? He held her fast, crooning *nena, nena, nena* as he had years ago with Luisa, until she caught her breath and scrubbed the tears away. An hour later, as they trudged through the sand to his pickup, she'd apologized for her outburst. He hoped like hell she'd forgiven him.

Pella had on more clothes this Monday morning, a stripped shirtwaist dress, sleeveless, but businesslike. She looked every bit as good to Hank as she had on the beach.

"Rhys came by for you this morning?"

Pella wrinkled her sunburned nose. "Oh, yes, Marshal. Everyone is obeying your orders."

"Things are quiet today. Roger's not here?"

"He's in Phoenix at Greenwood Development. The courses are closed on Monday and the realtors try to lay off after their busy weekend."

"Has he calmed down now that the greens are repaired?"

"Not much." Pella's gray eyes lost their smile. "They're all scared, Hank. Two more families announced at the cocktail party last night that they're putting their houses up for sale."

"How about you? Are you scared?"

She stared up at him, a defiant look. Then she reached into the open collar of her dress and pulled out the new siren pendant. "Sufficiently. The back entrance of this place is bolted. Ignacio and Luis will be working on the front garden all morning, checking out the visitors."

¡Gracios a Dios! She's decided to be sensible, Hank thought. "Roger's orders?"

"The one thing they can't afford is a body on their doorstep. That would cause a stampede." Her hair slid over her eyes as she examined her fingernails. "Their sales depend on ambiance. Exclusiveness, protection, status. You know – neighborhood, neighborhood, neighborhood. The residents don't know where this guy will strike next. They figure Greenwood sold them a lie when they told them this was a worry-free community. They were promised a permanent vacation, with nothing to do but play golf and party. That seems to be over."

"Families are putting their houses up for sale? What's Greenwood Development expecting?"

"A run on the bank. A panic virus passed from resident to resident." Pella rolled her chair back and stood up. "I've been studying Greenwood's balance sheet, Hank. Sonoran Skyline is their prime property and the five-year projections for profit are fantastic. But the other developments aren't doing well. The ones in California and Utah are smaller and not as fancy, plus they're too far from a city. If Sonoran Skyline is discredited, the whole corporation could be in big trouble."

"Could a competitor take advantage of the water situation to take over?"

"If this continues, it will do them in, competitor or not. That's another reason why Roger's so upset. He's invested his own savings in the venture."

Sanchez walked to the curved windows overlooking the restored green on the renamed Sacred Stone Golf Course. The county police had the report he'd written about the sprinkler re-programming. They had been mildly interested. The attack on Pella had been dismissed as not connected, so that was still his exclusive problem. Ditto the drowned dog. What Pella just said made sense. At least it was a new angle.

"Have there been any offers to buy the corporation?" He turned back to Pella.

"Not that I've heard, but that's likely secret information." She gave a bitter little chuckle. "You might've noticed that I'm not highly placed in this organization."

He gazed out the window again, hands in his pockets, jiggling his change. One of the greens keepers was mowing the fairway, taking large swaths with a machine that scooped up the clippings. Another man used an edge trimmer around the feet of a stone bench. Everything here was high-end, as close as humans could manage to paradise in the desert.

He wondered if the maintenance people had been able to dissolve the paint sprayed on the rough surface of that bench. He couldn't see any red from where he stood. The letters and numbers hadn't struck any sparks with anyone. "Is 411718." A cryptic question? All the officers agreed that 17 minus 18 didn't make 41. Neither did 17 plus 18, so the answer was no. The stone bench weighed too much to carry off as evidence, but the decoding expert on the county staff had been given a series of photos, and chips of the paint had been chiseled off for analysis.

He strolled back to the desk, picked up his hat and smiled at Pella, remembering the way she looked at the lake in her *traje de baño de azul.* For the time being his concentration was needed in other directions. "I'll be back to get you at lunchtime."

"Right." She gave a little shrug that had resignation scrawled all over it. "Five days until the festival. The wild excitement builds! Anyway, I've got an afternoon of details to pursue. Oh, Maud asked me to find her a few extra stagehands. A dum-dum job for guys with muscles who can take directions." She cocked an eyebrow, grinning as she looked him over. "Can you take directions? The Friday night performance."

"Will you be there?"

"Sure. Lining up tiny palo verde trees and cactus wrens for their first fling at stardom."

"Then I'll be there."

Outside he strolled down the path to join the two gardeners taking a break in the shade of a mesquite tree, their hands clutching half-gallon containers of Coke. "Luis, I hear you and Ignacio are undercover guards," he said in Spanish.

"*Si,*" Luis chuckled. "Today we are only disguised as gardeners. Sadly, the pay is the same. So is the work." He lifted the plastic bottle to his lips, took a couple of deep swigs and scrubbed his mouth with the back of his hand. "Is that your lady in there, Marshal? You are one lucky man."

Sanchez stared through the imposing two-story windows at Pella sitting alone at her desk in the huge reception room, the light shining on her golden head as she bent over her work. "More mine than anyone else's," he said, frowning, "Sure. Mine." He gripped the man's shoulder. "Take good care of her, Luis."

The marshal, phone to his ear, was discussing the progress of the Sonoran Skyline investigation with County Detective Sergeant Harvey Lubeck, when Linda buzzed through to him from her switchboard. Lubeck, Chuparrosa's usual contact with the Sheriff's Office, was an easygoing man with a steady eye for details. His expert advice, when Sanchez was the new kid on the block in Chuparrosa, had eased the marshal's first couple of months. The man treated him as an equal, and associate, and never minced words.

An hour earlier, Pella had been safely delivered to the festival headquarters across the courtyard from Hank's office. With his back door open, he had a clear view of all visitors who might come to her door. The heat gusting in from outside, along with bougainvillea blossoms, leaves from the carob tree and the occasional cactus wren, was uncomfortable, but he wouldn't miss any calls for help.

"Excuse me, Marshal." Linda's voice, crackling through the speakerphone, sounded unlike her. "Mr. Milford Wheat is here and wants to know if you have time to see him." There was a mumbling in the background. "W-what?" she said and giggled. "Oh, and Mr. Packard Wheat is here, too."

Hank wound up his conversation with Lubeck and strolled out to shake hands with Ford Wheat. The man stood in the middle of the front office, leaning on the counter that separated Linda's workstation from the rest of the room. A flame-colored tee shirt drooped off his narrow shoulders and stretched over his belly. His calfless legs jutted below plaid shorts. He put a fat paw in the marshal's hand, grinning up at him, his blue eyes alive with mischief.

"I brought someone for you to meet, Marshal." He checked over his shoulder. "Now where did he go?" There was a murmur behind him and Wheat reached between his legs to pull a child forward. "Ah, here he is. My grandson, Packard Wheat. We call him Packy."

He extended the child's limp arm so Hank could shake his hand, a boy of five or six, slender to the point of emaciation, peering shyly. His hair, badly cut, hung to the bridge of his freckled nose and tickled his prominent ears. His knees were knobs on spindly legs. The only plump things about the child were the padded sneakers he wore.

It was clear they wanted to talk. Sanchez ushered them into his office, where Wheat dropped onto a chair, and pulled Packy into the space between his knees, an arm around his narrow chest. He smoothed the slack brown hair off the boy's forehead and heaved a sigh.

"Packy arrived last night. Non-stop from New York."

"Did you fly by yourself, Packy?" Hank asked. He knew kids liked to tell their own stories.

Under his grandfather's hand the child seemed to be shaking his head "no."

"Of course he did, the brave lad. And he had a beautiful stewardess taking care of him." The hand gripped tighter, tugging the boy's head against Wheat's shoulder, stopping the movement. "His mother is off for a holiday in the Greek Isles. Packy'll stay with me for the school year. Today I'm taking him to meet the important people in town." Wheat's ruddy face broke into circling grooves as he smiled. "We've been to see the mayor, and after we talk to you, we have to meet the owner of the ice cream store. What's his name?"

"Josh Cooper."

"That's the man." He lifted the boy onto his knee. "We may open a charge account."

A suggestion of a smile flitted across Packy's face, and he swiveled his head to stare at Hank with frank, wide-open brown eyes. Does the kid have a voice, Hank wondered, and tried again.

"Will you go to public school, Packy, or private?"

"Oh, I've hired a tutor for him," chirped his grandfather. "He's getting a late start on first grade. It's already the end of September. We'll find a school for him when he's caught up." He gave the boy a squeeze and lifted him onto his knee. "We're creating a captain of industry here. First grade is just step one. Grandfather's only a Ford, but this kid's a Packard." Wheat laughed, set the child's huge sneakers back on the floor and gave him a playful shove. "Scoot out to the courtyard, buddy. I want to talk to the marshal."

Packy ran toward the open door, his knees knocking together, rubber soles squeaking over the floor tiles. They watched him stumble across the gravel to the carob tree, where he began picking apart one of the seedpods that littered the ground.

"He's a stoic little asthma sufferer, you know." Wheat's shock of fuzzy white hair quivered as he shook his head. "Can't indulge in strenuous activity, but he's bright and loves to read, so we keep him busy. His mother, bless her, drops in now and again, but he's really more my child than hers. We changed his name to 'Wheat' after her last divorce." He shifted his feet and craned his neck to watch the boy stuffing carob pods in the pockets of his khaki shorts.

"Now, Marshal, I need your indulgence with a surprise." Milford Wheat's eyes disappeared in the furrows of his smile as he beamed again. "I have arranged to present a fireworks display on Saturday night following the pageant. Nothing lavish, you understand. A twenty minute show to celebrate the founding of my new home town." He set his hands on his knees and leaned forward to receive Hank's applause. "What do you think of that, huh?"

"Mr. Wheat, those arrangements take a long time to make. Have you talked to Pella? Where do you plan to launch the show? How about the permits?"

"Now, no need to panic. I ran the idea past Mel Bergen first. When he liked it, I got the county permit and signed a contract for the display. Greenwood Development has agreed to let us use some bladed ground on the Chuparrosa side of Sonoran Skyline. It's between the club house and Buckskin Road." He rubbed his hands together. "It's for the kids, of course, mine and everybody else's. This is going to be a fantastic festival. I want it to finish with a big bang."

Sanchez bent to dig in a drawer for the proper city forms to cover an event like this. He knew the doubts he felt showed in his face. The tension in town was explosive enough without adding Wheat's pyrotechnics. Problems had stretched his staff to their limits. Every one of them was working overtime, with worse to come on festival weekend. They couldn't be everywhere. But Wheat's planning had neatly tied his hands, and the little guy was so damned pleased with himself.

"How did you do this so fast, Mr. Wheat? These displays usually take weeks to set up. Permits take time to process."

"No problemo, señor. I've procured permits all over the known world in my time, for things you wouldn't believe you'd need permits for. There are a hundred ways to grease the skids, and I invented most of 'em." He chuckled, groped in the pocket of his shorts for a handkerchief and patted his brow. "September is a slack season for the fireworks companies. I found one with enough rockets on hand for the small production I had in mind. The technicians are hired and glad to have the work. I'm picking up the tab for all of it."

"Did you say you'd talked to Pella?" Something wasn't quite right in this snow job. He wondered why the mayor had given his approval. Was it a bit of fence mending to make Greenwood Development look like jolly good fellows?

"Sure. Gave her the glad news by phone just before I came to see you. You think she's still at the Skyline office? Packy and I'll mosey that way in a few minutes and fill in the details."

It seemed the deed was as good as done. The marshal was the last to know. "If you'll bring the contract and permit in tomorrow, we can fill out the city's forms. You've read the stipulations for certified technicians? Then what else would you like the marshal's office to do?"

"Crowd control. Keep the kids off Sonoran Skyline property for the evening. You know how kids are. Parents don't always control 'em. We'll be located a bit northeast of the clubhouse in an area of rough. I expect cars will be parked on Buckskin Trail and Apache Boot Wash Road, but most folks can watch from their homes. Spanish Saddle Mountain would be a great viewing spot."

Wheat pushed his hands hard against his knees, bent forward and uncurled into an upright position. "Roger Martineau is awfully pleased about the fireworks display, I can tell you. He had to be in on it, of course. Thinks it will project Sonoran Skyline's image of corporate concern for the whole community." He stepped to the open door and cupped his hands around his mouth to hail the child in the courtyard. "Hey, Packy, let's walk on over to see the ice cream man. Well, I wonder where my boy has gotten himself off to."

The plaza appeared to be empty as Sanchez stood up to usher his guest out the back door. He and Wheat crunched over the gravel to the carob tree, peering up and down the silent place. Entrances leading to other city offices in the quadrangle were closed. A walkway through a single arch at the end of the colonnade led to the street.

"Packy!" Wheat called. "He could have gotten out of here by himself. With all the strange goings on in town, I should have kept him with me. I thought...I mean, a park right outside the marshal's office..."

A hiccup made Sanchez look into the dense foliage above. Packy's dark eyes shone out among the green leaves. He clung to the trunk of the huge tree with slender arms, legs curled rigidly onto an extended branch.

"Packy, you young scoundrel," his grandfather yelled. "Jump down here this instant, or you'll get no ice cream. Why didn't you answer when I called?"

"I can't." The boy's voice sounded faint and despairing.

Hank stepped onto the bench that circled the tree and the child slowly released his grip to slide into his arms, relaxing against his chest, hiccupping and trembling. "How long were you up there?" He set Packy on the ground and crouched to look at him, his hands on the boy's shaking shoulders. "Are you okay, buddy?"

"He's right as rain, Marshal. Always one for adventure." Wheat was smiling again, reaching for the child's hand, drawing him out of Hank's grasp. "Easier to go up than down, eh? Remember that next time. And answer when you're called." He moved with quick strides toward the arch that led to Gold Dust Avenue, pulling Packy along.

The boy trotted behind at his clumsy gate, stumbling in the big sneakers, head hanging. His voice of protest was low but distinct. "I forgot my name was Packy," he said.

Chapter 13

"So what's wrong with a few fireworks?" Mel Bergen demanded and slammed his mug down on the desk. A splash of coffee spread in an irregular pattern across the blotter. He pushed his spectacles up and glared at Hank Sanchez, who stood with his back against the wall in the small office.

A shaft of sunlight sliced between them through the open door. Outside, in the courtyard, house finches celebrated a bright Tuesday morning with bursts of song. Inside the mayor defended his opinion with all the bravado of a man stuck with a bad decision.

"The timing, for one thing," Sanchez said. "The chance for more violence at Sonoran Skyline, for another." He understood that Bergen had given his word to a worthy citizen, but any fool could see problems here. He wanted to lay out all the possibilities before they happened. And he wanted a contingency plan for handling each one. "We've been rushed into this. I don't like the location…"

"It's a done deal, I tell you." With a flip of his hand, Bergen dismissed all Hank's objections. "Absolutely *fait accompli*. Other towns have fireworks displays. You'll just have to deal with it."

Sunday and Monday had gone by without a crime against Sonoran Skyline. Two days and holding. Had the perpetrator left town? Hank's intuition told him that a pause in the siege didn't mean the war was over. The crimes were becoming more destructive, and the marshal's office couldn't begin to cover the additional thirty six hundred acres that made up the whole development. In Chuparrosa alone, their resources were stretched. He scowled and flexed his shoulders against the wall, thinking about the potential for catastrophe given the dark night, a rally of rockets, a crew of strangers.

"A fireworks display means hours of set-up time, with a bunch of workers milling around. The safety precautions alone are staggering, and only a reputable business can be trusted to do it right. They're not talking about lighting a few sparklers. A twenty minute display will involve an enormous amount of gunpowder."

The mayor reached for the coffee pot, his jaw clenched, mouth a stubborn line. "We can trust Ford Wheat to do this right. Your job is to get him fixed up legally and help him with the crowds of delighted citizens on Saturday night."

Being a wealthy golfer didn't automatically bestow nobility on the man, Hank thought. There was good deal at stake here. "What do we know about Mr. Wheat, Mel?"

The harsh lines in Bergen's face softened into a smug smile. "Had him vetted by an east coast friend of mine, a lawyer I've known for years. Apparently Wheat has a reputation as a deal maker. He puts things together and lets other people run them. Stays in the background, you know. He has the golden touch, with business ventures on every continent. Travels most of the year. Now he's decided to settle down, which is a blessing for Chuparrosa! With all that executive ability and money, he can do this town an enormous amount of good."

Sanchez frowned and considered this news. "Your friend the lawyer, he knows him personally?"

"Well, only hearsay, but he's checked him out. Wheat's a behind-the-scenes kind of operator. Low profile. Hey, you've talked to the man. You gotta love a guy who'll take on a grandson with never a word against the kid's jet set mother. I'll bet he even sends her flowers on Mother's Day." Bergen raised a bushy eyebrow and smoothed one hand over the damp splotches on his blotter. "If he can locate her."

"He's coming in today with his permit and contract. I can't object if they're in order, but my deputies will be overworked this weekend, as it is. I'll have to hire some extra people."

The mayor rubbed his chin. "Send your boys home after the rodeo, and I'll volunteer the city council as your crowd control. Dig out those orange vests you bought and tell us what to do."

Sanchez glanced out the door at a mourning dove fluttering in the fountain and thought about the members of Chuparrosa city council. Two middle-aged women. Five men, one in a wheelchair, all pushing seventy. "Mel...ah, why don't we give the guys a break during the daytime, instead. I'll plan a schedule for the council so they can work the craft show, the rodeo and the old settler's picnic. Linda'll bring it over to you later this morning."

The mayor's frown lightened. "Fine," he said. "Put me down for the picnic since I'll be there anyway. Say, is there any chance you could get those pickets to lay off over Friday and Saturday? A scragglier looking bunch of cowboys I never saw. Candidates for skin cancer, every one of 'em."

"We can't violate their right to assemble."

Bergen's expression said that he could. "Well, have a talk with them and see what you can do. It's for the good of the town, after all. Show a little civic pride and all that." He scratched one ear and shook his head in bewilderment. "I've played many golf games with Bud Brickson. I thought he had more sense."

The marshal had sent Linda Smallseed off to the mayor's office about noon with the patrol schedule for the city council, when Kevin Dingle clattered up to his door.

"Pella's settled safe and sound in the festival office for the afternoon. She didn't mind that you were too busy to pick her up," he said, bending his agile body around the doorframe. "We stopped at the yogurt shop for her lunch. She doesn't eat enough, but she said not to worry about her."

The reports and photos of the damaged golf courses, hot off the computer from the county police, were spread out on Hank's desk, where he had been comparing them with the shots he had taken himself. He raised his head, hiding the interest he felt in Pella's safety. "No new complaints from Soronan Skyline?"

"They asked me to moonlight as their night guard in that clubhouse construction site for the rest of this week. I said I could if you didn't object."

Sanchez glanced back at his large, black and white photo of the bench with the strange message. The picture, taken on Saturday, showed Roger in the background talking to a cluster of golfers. Two couples in shorts sat in their carts. Farther back, stood a man in jeans and mirror sunglasses. All, except the bench, were out of focus, features blurred. Sunglasses might be one of the grounds crew. His appearance seemed more like a cowboy, though, narrow and wiry. Even in the grainy background of the picture, there was a coiled-spring quality about the man.

"I can't spare you on Friday in the daytime and Saturday, all day and all night," said Hank. "That's going to be a long, tough duty. Milford Wheat is planning a fireworks display out at Sonoran Skyline on Saturday night. We'll all have to be there."

Kevin slouched toward the desk, a grin on his freckled face. "Fireworks! Sure, I'll tell them I have to work there." He hesitated, hands in his pockets, his jaw revolving on a wad of gum. "You know, the pickets are still out in force. I hadn't driven by there for a couple days. They have new signs."

Hank nodded. "I saw them yesterday. Is Sugar the artist? She's got a great talent for cartooning. Martineau's blood pressure must shoot up every time he sees those pictures of himself."

"I guess Sugar did the first ones, but these are better." The boy waggled his head. "I thought you might want to know. It makes me wonder if Isaiah Morley's back in town."

"Another Morley prophet? Who the hell is he?"

"You haven't been here long enough." Kevin reached for the coffee pot, measured out half a cup, added creamer and dropped into the guest chair. "He's the Morley's oldest son. He must be like..." The calculations made his eyes squint. "...twenty seven."

"Where's he been?" Hank was indeed interested. A large part of Kevin's value to the Chuparrosa marshal's office was the fact that he'd been born twenty-one years before on the edge of town, and he knew everyone. Not just the people who'd been in town for three decades, he knew all the people who'd arrived since. A gossipy kid with an innocent face, he could draw out the most reserved new resident. He was a walking-talking file of long forgotten tidbits, facts and speculations. When dredged up, they could add color to any individual profile. His observations tended to be accurate.

Kevin shrugged. "They don't ever talk about him much. He got into trouble at school when he was seventeen. He and Butch had a row over it, and he cleared out. He's hot tempered like his dad, but small like Sugar. I heard he got the worst of it from Butch."

"And he drew cartoons?"

"Did he ever." Kevin snickered. "He sneaked into the school one night and painted pictures of his teachers all over the walls. They were great caricatures. He ruined several reputations. I remember he drew the principal grabbing money out of the safe, and a couple of teachers in the sack together. One was abusing some kid. No doubt about which teachers he was accusing. Butch thought it was a riot when Isaiah got expelled. Then the Morleys got the bill for the cleanup, and ol' dad started bouncing junior off the walls."

"A guy with his own brand of social justice, I take it. So where's he been for ten years?"

"Not here. Jerry told me once that he was in Montana workin' on a ranch." Kevin rearranged his feet and stared out the window. "There was always a wild streak in Isaiah. I don't know. Vicious? Kids my age admired him because of the trouble he caused, but we stayed out of his way."

"Would you know him if you saw him now?"

Dingle tossed his empty coffee cup in the trash basket. "Sure. He has those aquamarine eyes. Just like Sugar's. That glassy color of water in a swimming pool."

Sanchez studied the photo on his desk once more, the cowboy loitering in the distance, the hard black lettering on the bench. As Kevin turned to go, the marshal reached for the phone and left three messages, one a request for a call-back from the county sheriff's office, one a research question for Janet Peterson at the Chuparrosa library and one for the CEO of Greenwood Development, asking for an urgent meeting.

An hour later the marshal's patrol car was climbing the twisty gravel road that led up Spanish Saddle Mountain. Before leaving he had gone to a great deal of trouble to lure Pella across the courtyard into the safety of his own office. She'd laughed at him for his foolishness, but agreed at last that she could do her work there until he returned. He'd bolted the back door.

In his rearview mirror he caught a glimpse of the pickets gathered at the bottom of the hill, their shapes filtered through the cloud of dust trailing his car. He'd stopped to examine the new signs, planted like a border of fancy flowers along the road. Made of plywood, cleated onto stakes, they were too heavy to carry off, able to withstand wind and rain. Permanent signs. The cartoons were wicked pictures of Martineau, one with a fire hose shooting water on downtown Chuparrosa and another of him tiptoeing off with petroglyphs. On some, golfers were clubbing hikers and people on horseback. He picked out the unmistakable likenesses of the mayor and the council members among the golfers.

Micah Morley, a gimme cap from Howling Coyote Feed Store backwards on his low brow, clenched his fists as Hank walked the row of artwork. Fiesta Flores danced toward him, pulling off her floppy gold sombrero to use as a fan. She begged Hank to arrest her and take her off to a nice air-conditioned jail. To one side leaning against the solitary mesquite tree, Bud Brickson gave every indication of wanting to be someplace else.

"The mayor hopes you'll be willing to put away your signs for the two days of the festival," Hank had said.

"Damn right he does." Micah's jaw jutted forward in an ugly smile as he rocked back on his heels. "But we got the media comin'."

Bud shifted his feet and looked uncomfortable. "Well, maybe."

"For sure!" Fiesta had clapped her hat back on at a saucy angle and favored Hank with her lovely smile. "I contacted some friends of mine. A couple of TV stations, newspaper reporters, photographers. Their camera crews'll be here Friday and Saturday for some extraordinary publicity."

Somewhere Sanchez had heard that there was no such thing as bad publicity, but he knew the mayor wouldn't believe that.

He continued the slow drive up Apache Boot until he reached the Morley's lane. He found some shade on the east side of the stable and stepped out into the settling dust.

The open arena seemed deserted, so he headed down the outside of the stable toward the paddock gate, past the half-doors, picture windows for the lucky horses whose owners could afford box stalls. In the dim light of the last stall he caught a glimpse of Zephyr Wilson's thin face. Her hair, pulled out of the neat braid, waved over her hunched shoulders, and in her eyes burned the panic of a hunted animal. As he walked toward her, he could see that the dark patches on her face weren't shadows, but bruises, shattering and deep.

She shut her eyes and gave a gasp. "I thought you were Jake," she breathed.

"God, Zephyr, you don't have to let Jake do that to you. We'll come out any time you need us. I'll find you another place to stay and help you move."

"I know." Her whisper rustled toward him through the dust motes hovering in the air. "I deserved it this time."

During the year that she and her lover, Jake Scarlett had rented the place next door to Morley's, the marshal's office had received at least half a dozen domestic violence calls from the neighbors. Each time the deputy had spent an hour calming Jake down and trying to persuade Zephyr to file charges, but it had been a lost cause. Battered, but loyal, that was Zephyr.

"Is that what Jake told you? *Muchacha,* nobody deserves a beating like you've taken." He looked her over, alarmed by the marks of savagery. Jake, who outweighed his girl friend by a hundred pounds, was mean even when cold sober. She was often bruised, but other times the man had been careful to spare her face. "Do you want me to talk to him? Have you seen a doctor?"

She shook her head a couple of times and retreated farther into the stall. "Sugar's down there." She pointed to the other end of the stable. "Watering the horses."

He let himself in the paddock gate, brushed through the milling crowd of horses and hiked the length of the building to the stall where Sugar was squirting water in a bucket. The lose horses trotted along behind him.

"Since you're here, you can tell those horses why all our water has to be saved for drinking." She didn't turn to face him. When the bucket was full, she crimped the hose and moved to the next stall.

A big bay nuzzled Hank's arm. He cupped his hand to caress the animal's nose and smoothed his sleek chestnut neck. One leg was bandaged below the hock. "Is this your horse, Sugar?"

She turned back, a dirty look at him, a soft one for the horse. "That's the Turk."

His hand slid over the Turk's neck again, his finger twisting around a long hair in his mane. An easy pull, and he pushed it into his pocket. The county lab could tell him if it matched the hairs he'd found on the wire fence that separated Sonoran Skyline from the national forest.

"What happened to his leg?"

Sugar compressed her mouth and shifted the dust as she yanked the hose to move to the next stall. Gripping the crimped hose, she turned to face him, her eyes turquoise slits. "What do you want here, Sanchez?"

"I came to talk to Isaiah. Know where I can find him?"

Her hand slipped on the hose and water dribbled onto the dirt between them before she tightened her grip. "He's in Utah. Cowboyin'. I don't know where."

"The pickets have clever new signs. I heard Isaiah painted them."

"No, I did . And you didn't come all the way up here to tell me you liked 'em. Get back in your car and leave us alone." She swung away from him to push the nozzle into another pail, the back of her hand scrubbing her cheeks.

"You know we have to find him, Sugar." He wasn't ready to threaten her just yet. He needed firmer ground. "I expect a call if you hear from Isaiah."

The marshal turned and retraced his steps to the paddock gate. Zephyr still hovered, waif-like, against the stall door, her brown eyes staring out of a face blank and blackened by blows from her lover's fists. Hank had to try again.

"Come back to the office with me, Zephyr, and file a complaint against Jake. A night or two in jail will make him stop and think."

She raised her eyes to his for only an instant before she shook her head. Wasn't she scared of Jake? She should be by now. There was a lifeless quality about her, as if she'd given up. Why did she say she deserved the beating this time?

The Turk nudged his shoulder again, then raised his nose higher and, like an expert, tipped Hank's broad-brimmed hat onto the dirt at Zephyr's feet. "Hey!" the marshal said and bent over to rescue it before the bay could plant a hoof on the brim.

Then he noticed Zephyr's small feet. In red cowgirl boots, with elaborate designs stitched in black and fake snakeskin tops. High-fashion boots, over-decorated, cheap. But it was the delicate size that interested him the most, the pointed toes and the narrow curved heels.

Chapter 14

At the bottom of the pool at the Sonoran Skyline clubhouse, far below the shining surface, lay a body, shifting listlessly in the still water. Roger Martineau, his knees slightly bent, stared with unblinking blue eyes toward the cool-deck, while his pale hair swayed like moss on a rock. Blood, flowing from the deep crimson slash below his chin, had tainted the clear liquid around his head a muddy gray. Overhead, in the fresh blue of the morning sky, a vulture wheeled closer and closer, alert to opportunities blown by the scent of death.

From the clubhouse, screams came whooping over and over. "No-o-o, no-o-o, no-o-o…!" High pitched, mechanical, as if someone had flipped a switch marked "anguish" and forgotten to turn it off. The sound flowed beyond the tinted glass doors of the central lounge to Marshal Sanchez, as he stood on the patio beside the Olympic-sized swimming pool.

He raised his head and frowned, thinking of Pella, who had dashed over at his call to calm a frenzied Luanne Martineau. It was clear that she wasn't having much luck.

On one bare section of the wall, where the bougainvillea had not yet fulfilled its potential, someone had spray painted a phrase like the one on the golf course bench. Only the numbers were different – Is431920. The splotch of graffiti must have been one of the last sights Roger Martineau saw, Hank thought. And it must have made him furious.

Sanchez began his third circle of the pool. It was shadowed, at this early morning hour, by the mesquite trees on the eastern edges of the cool deck. Six dense, mature trees, another sign that no expense had been spared a year and a half ago when clubhouse-number-one was built. The lush green plantings formed a tropical paradise that, like the golf courses, denied the desert lying just outside its walls.

Every inch of the thicket surrounding the pool would have to be searched for evidence, but for now he'd concentrate on the cool deck. Moving slowly, eyes on the ground, he jotted notes on a pad. He'd made a decent sketch of the scene for his own use and taken some photos. When the county "ident" team arrived with the consent-to-search form from Greenwood Development, they'd take over the formal investigation. As first on the scene, his job was to observe, not touch.

Patches of blood, splayed on one edge of the cool-deck, were drying in the hot sun. At the pool's lip some brownish spots had been splashed with water, forming diluted pink puddles. Sanchez stepped around them and took his time inspecting this part of the surface.

He had ordered the filtering system and the water feature, a solid wall on the west end of the long pool, turned off. The lavender tiled bulwark against the desert was losing its gloss as it dried. Whatever debris had been caught by the filter would be painstakingly picked over and preserved for analysis. Careful netting could capture anything else in the pool. The pad of six tennis courts on the west and other adjacent grounds should be checked, as well. The murderer must have arrived on foot across the golf courses. Clues to his identity could be scattered anywhere on the several thousand acres. With luck they'd pick up his trail and not be condemned to searching them all.

And where had the killer entered the pool area, Hank wondered? A gate in the wall, leading to the tennis courts, remained locked. There were no statues lying broken on the ground like the St. Francis he'd found in the Martineau's patio. This time the intruder had been more careful. As Sanchez peered beyond the wall at new plantings of shrubbery and bedding plants that softened the pink stucco, he considered the places where it would have been possible for an athletic person to hoist himself up to the top. The garden below had been mulched with pebbles. Not a promising medium for footprints.

Straightening up to begin his fourth circle, Sanchez noticed threads caught on one thorn of a mesquite, a few gray fibers at a spot where an intruder could have come tumbling off the wall. On the ground at his feet lay a broken cluster of the tree's fernlike leaves. He tagged the branch and kept walking.

Someone had hidden on the patio, waited for Roger, slit his throat and dumped him into the water. And not long ago, either. The blood beside the pool was still sticky, even in the low humidity of a September morning. Had Roger's killer been trained in commando tactics? Puddles of water on the cool deck suggested that he might have jumped in the pool afterwards to erase all traces of blood on his clothing and hands. Then he'd vanished, unnoticed. A quiet time, the hours between four and six in the morning. The patrols were out, but a lone man could evade them with ease in the predawn gloom. Hell, they'd missed two horses on Friday night.

At least the golf course vandalism had served some sort of insane purpose. It called attention to the town's water problems and showed contempt for the development. Roger's grisly death was an act of terrorism. Like a poker player's desperate raise, it jacked up the stakes far out of proportion to the original ante. But the killer was bluffing. Hank knew his hand wasn't all that great.

Sonoran Skyline had been handicapped by their denial. They had believed that with a wave of their hand they could dismiss the water problems, the needs of others, the anger in the community and all the obstacles would vanish. They had refused to acknowledge any harm in replacing the ancient desert with an imported environment.

Through the sliding glass doors Sanchez could see three employees who had found Martineau's body. They were seated in a row on one of the bright sofas in the clubhouse lounge, their faces pale and sober from the shock of their discovery. Deputy Dingle had taken separate statements before they'd had a chance to compare notes. Alfredo Diaz and Pablo Salado, gardeners, had peeped over the wall when they came to work at five thirty. Young Joey Lister, kitchen helper, had stumbled into the patio for a smoke after the gardeners ran for help. Now they waited for the county people to interrogate them, huddled together, enduring Luanne's expression of fury at the world.

For a moment, sirens outside the building drowned out the sounds of her grief. Dingle disappeared in the direction of the porte-cochere. After a few minutes, Detective Harvey Lubeck lumbered onto the patio followed by a three-person 'ident' team burdened with cameras and equipment. The new arrivals hung around the pool staring at the submerged corpse while Sanchez briefed them.

"Jeeze, thirty six hundred acres!" snorted the man with the camera. "Hope I've got enough film."

They scattered to begin their work. Lubeck stayed behind, his quiet eyes following the sunbeams as they glanced off the water.

"Mrs. Martineau?" With a grimace he flicked his head in the direction of the wailing. "That's going to drive us all batty. The ME'S on his way and a delegation from Greenwood should be here any minute." Lubeck turned back to Hank and scratched the bald spot on the top of his head. "Any theories?"

Sanchez shook his head. None that he was ready to share just yet. The day before he had requested and received from Lubeck the FBI report on Isaiah Morley. Lubeck would have checked that over, too. The contract Chuparrosa had with the county to provide services during a serious crime allowed the detective to run the show. The marshal was comfortable with that for the time being.

"Alfredo Diaz called the office about five-forty yelling that he and Pablo Salado had seen Martineau's body in the pool." Sanchez waved toward the glass doors. "They're ready to be interviewed."

"Weapons? Blood?"

"Not on them. They'd come through the main gate five minutes before and hightailed it back there to phone."

Lubeck began to take notes in an offhand way, keeping watch on the photographer in case he needed direction. "Pella came with you?"

"I asked Kevin to pick her up. Luanne needed a companion."

"Nice guy. You gave her the tough job."

They circled the pool, Lubeck making notes and talking steadily. "You requested information on a man named Isaiah Morley. A suspect?"

"Damned if I know. I heard his name for the first time yesterday. No one in Chuparrosa has seen him, and his mother says he's in Utah."

"I see you've got another message to decode." Lubeck pointed his pen at the wall of graffiti and studied Sanchez with narrowed eyes. "Our guys haven't had any luck."

Hank shrugged. The day before he'd called Janet Peterson at the library to ask if they had a copy of the Bible. She'd read out the verses he wanted in her clear librarian voice and then paused. "You know, Marshal, I'm a lifetime Lutheran, but I don't think I've ever read those verses before today," she said. "Isaiah 41: 17-18. They're...so... applicable, aren't they? 'When the poor and needy seek water and there is none, and their tongue is parched with thirst, I, the Lord, will answer them.' And then this next verse is about opening rivers on the bare heights. 'I will make the wilderness a pool of water, and the dry land springs of water.' It's amazing."

Sanchez had agreed with her, thanked her and hung up the phone. Did a present-day Isaiah believe he was the Lord's anointed on a holy mission? It was a chilling glimpse into the man's mind. Did it explain his justification for murder? The first chance he had, he'd call Janet back and ask her to look up the new reference. Then he'd send an e-mail to the detective's office.

Lubeck yanked off his sunglasses to examine the threads Hank had tagged on the mesquite. "Here's where he came in. I'd bet on it." He made more swift notes and beckoned the photographer over to take a picture. Then he replaced the glasses and turned his gaze to the body below in the water. "You want this Isaiah picked up?"

Hank cleared his throat. He knew he stood on shaky ground. "The report said Morley is a trained eco-terrorist. He served time in Oregon for 'monkey wrenching.' Spiking trees and pouring sand in the gas tanks of bulldozers. He's suspected of trying to sabotage a nuclear facility. If he's in Chuparrosa, he's probably in violation of parole."

Lubeck nailed Sanchez with a steely glance. "Have we got enough for a search warrant for the Morley place?"

"What's the probable cause? He hasn't been seen. He grew up here and knows a hundred places to hole up in the back country beyond Morley's."

"A terrorist." Lubeck squinted above the trees where the persistent vulture glided on an updraft.

"Eco…," Sanchez corrected. He knew what was coming, and he didn't want to hear it.

"You know, Hank, if there's a chance he's involved, we have to give the FBI a call," Lubeck said. "Anyway, for now we'll check on his parole status and see if he's still in Utah or Oregon. Too bad there weren't any unknown fingerprints on that butcher paper you picked up on Martineau's patio. We'll get a print record in case he's left one here."

The morning had worn on to nine o'clock by the time Hank trotted up the steps of Martineau's home to press the bell beside the double doors. Pella opened one and gave him a goofy smile.

"Are you all right?" He put his hands on her shoulders and searched her face.

"Uh huh. Who would have thought Luanne had such well-developed lungs? I found her a tranquilizer and she's resting."

"Asleep? I wanted a word with her."

"Her son's with her in her room. This is ghastly for him, too. I've been calling a list of people she asked me to notify. Some of them said they'd be right out, so we'll be having company any minute. How's the investigation going?"

"Too soon to tell." He shook his head. "There's nothing like a murder to get the attention of the county police. They'll be swarming over the place all day. How did you get her to come home?"

"After sympathy and a glass of brandy failed, I told her that the press would be here any minute, and didn't she want to freshen up."

"Good call. They're beating on the doors to the clubhouse now. Will you tell her I need a statement before they get here?"

Pella's sandals clattered down the length of pink marble hall and in a few minutes a subdued looking Luanne appeared. She'd changed into a creamy silk blouse and slacks. Her hair was pulled back with a bow, but her face, under its smooth tan, appeared splotchy from weeping. With a wan smile she led him into the parlor, indicated a chair, and sank onto the white leather sofa.

"If I tell you what I know, will you tell me what you've found out?" she asked.

Sanchez flipped open a notebook. "Routine stuff, Mrs. Martineau. It doesn't mean a thing. We won't have any kind of analysis for several days. What was your husband doing at the clubhouse so early in the morning?"

She sucked in her breath, eyes closed, then exhaled. "He'd gotten a call. We were still in bed, naturally, and it woke us. About five o'clock."

"Who called?"

"Alfredo Diaz." She twisted a lace-edged hanky. "He's one of the gardeners."

"Did you answer the phone? Did you hear him speak?"

She shook her head. "Roger answered. After he hung up, he jumped out of bed and began to grab his clothes. He said Alfredo told him that someone had spray-painted swear words all over the patio at the clubhouse."

"And he was headed there to check it out?"

"He was livid." Luanne closed her eyes again. "He's been in torment ever since these water people started harassing us. He couldn't believe an honest businessman in this country should have to put up with that kind of abuse. He was so sure the police would take care of it, would protect us."

Sanchez ignored the jabs. "He told you he was going to the clubhouse?"

"Yes. He knew he'd have to have it cleaned off or painted over right away. He couldn't let the members wander into that unpleasantness. There are water aerobic classes this morning, people have lunch by the pool. There wasn't much time."

"What time did he leave the house? Did he walk or drive?"

"He took the car." She raised her eyes to the window. The clubhouse sprawled in the distance, on the other side of the eighth fairway. "He always drove. Always in a hurry."

"And the time he left?"

"It was still dark in the bedroom. I looked at the clock when the phone rang. It said 5:02. It couldn't have been later than 5:15."

"Did Roger say why the gardeners had come to work before daylight?"

Luanne stared down at her hands pulling at the fabric of her hankie. "No…no…he didn't question that. He just reacted to more bad news."

"Was Roger involved financially in Sonoran Skyline?"

Her face crumpled, and she covered it with her hands. "Greenwood let us buy $750,000 worth of private stock. Everything we had. It seemed like such a sure thing, so safe. And Roger got a good job along with it. The house." Her voice grew more muffled. "Why are they trying to ruin us?"

A phone rang down the hall, and when they heard Pella's footsteps on the marble tiles, Luanne turned, her face anxious. "That must be my sister," she said and ran out of the room.

Pella stuck her head around the corner. "Bad timing?"

Sanchez stood up and walked to the front door. "No. I got all the answers I need for the moment. I can find you a lift home. Or are you staying?"

"Till the friends arrive. It shouldn't be long. I've got plenty to do on the festival this afternoon." She paused, doubtful. "You don't think they'll cancel it, do you?"

"Probably not. You've given it a momentum of its own." He considered a moment, frowning, wondering if another warning would scare her or just make her rebellious. "That could have been you in the pool."

Her gray eyes widened, then she caught her breath and grinned. "Not bloody likely. I have this bodyguard who won't let me out of his sight."

"Right. Let's keep it that way." He ignored an urge to ravish her on the pink marble floor and settled for a kiss. "I'm going back to the clubhouse. Kevin or I will come for you at noon. Don't let in anyone you don't know!"

Milford Wheat stamped like an angry bull, glaring at the don't-cross ribbons, a flimsy yellow fence shutting off his entrance to the clubhouse. He seemed unaware that he was clutching Packy's skinny wrist in one plump paw, or that the child's frightened eyes were glued to his face.

Their Rolls was parked at the far end of the double column of emergency vehicles stretching the length of the driveway. They'd hiked from there, and Wheat had ordered that the marshal be found and delivered to the spot. By the time Hank received the message and was able to get away, the top of Wheat's baldhead was wet with perspiration and the child's head drooped hopelessly.

"What's going on in there?" Wheat demanded as the marshal came into view. It was a side of the man Sanchez hadn't seen before. A hard-jawed stranger with eyes like flints had replaced the jovial grandfather.

"Good morning, Mr. Wheat. Packy." Hank tousled the boy's hair and felt him pull back. "We're investigating an apparent homicide."

"Martineau?"

"Afraid so."

Their eyes locked for a moment and Hank watched, puzzled, as the man choked down his rage. Hell, he and Martineau had met only three weeks ago. Or had the two men known each other before? Some place else, some other time?

Packy began to whimper and pull at the hand gripping his wrist. "That hurts. Leggo!"

The child peeled back his grandfather's fingers one by one, ducked under the yellow ribbon and scampered toward the clubhouse. He disappeared around the northern corner with Hank in hot pursuit. Wheat, restrained from following by the patrolman, swore at them in impotent bellows.

Around the corner, Sanchez found himself in another artificial forest glen between the main clubhouse dining room and the tenth hole of Ocotillo Course. Packy's oversized sneakers had carried him to the edge of the fairway. The boy cast a worried glance over his shoulder and ran out to the middle of the grassy expanse where he paused, skittish as a bird.

There had been times in Hank's youth when he had spent hours chasing horses through pastures. He had learned, at last, that if he relaxed under a tree, with his hat pulled down to his chin, curiosity would get the better of the frisky animal. Soon it would come loping over to knock the hat off and stick its docile nose into the halter. In the knot of shade from a rustling palm, Hank lowered himself onto the heels of his boots and began juggling three small pebbles.

The child on the fairway hunkered down on his haunches, watching for a couple moments. Then he began to crawl toward the marshal on all fours like a stalking cat.

When he reached the rough, Packy sat down, arms clutching grass-stained knees and regarded Sanchez with solemn dark eyes.

"Are you gonna take me back to Grandpa?"

"Where do you want to go, Packy?"

"Home." There was a tremor in the boy's voice.

"Your grandpa's house?"

"Where I was before I came on the airplane."

"How can we find that place?"

Packy shut his eyes and screwed up his face as tears rolled down his cheeks. "I don't know," he mumbled.

Sanchez moved toward him and stretched out at an unthreatening level on the grass. "Did someone come with you on the plane, Packy?"

Sniffling, the youngster rubbed his nose with one fist before he opened his eyes, still shiny with tears. "Yeah. A guy."

"Did he have a name? What did you call him?"

The six-year-old pulled the bottom of his tee shirt up to his face to scrub at the tears, muffling the whispered word.

"Tell me again."

"Izzy." Now the boy seemed scared. "He told me not to tell. He said if I did, he'd hold my head in the toilet."

"I won't tell him you told me. Everybody's got to have a name." Sanchez stood up, lifted Packy in his arms and began to walk at a comfortable pace in the direction of the front entrance. Maybe the kid's Puerto Rican, he thought, and tried some Spanish. *"¿Como se llama, nino?"* No glimmer of understanding lit the child's face, so he repeated the question in English. "What was your name before you came here?"

"Josef."

"And you lived with your mother?"

"With Mama Grace."

The small arm tightened around Hank's neck as they came to the corner of the clubhouse, where they could see Ford Wheat pawing the ground, his angry eyes skewering the officer who refused to let him cross the tape. He dredged up a smile as he reached to claim Packy/ Josef, still clinging to Sanchez.

"Packy, you rascal, haven't I told you to stay with me? He's not a naughty boy, Marshal, just high spirited." The questioning eyes met Hank's, measured his suspicions, and appeared satisfied. "His mother, my daughter, was the same – always testing. She went to three private schools before we found one that could handle her."

"Have you found a housekeeper, Mr. Wheat?"

The man raised his eyebrows. "Sure. I hired a woman named Elena Salado. We'll keep her on, if she works out and Packy likes her."

"Pablo Salado's wife?"

"Pablo? I thought she said her husband's name was Julio." Wheat gave a disinterested shrug and set the child's feet on the ground, one hand again locked liked a cuff around his wrist. "Come on, Packy, let's go find a box of grape Popsicles.

Sanchez watched the pair walk back to the Rolls, Ford Wheat striding with purpose, Packy, his knees knocking together, struggling to keep up. For some crazy reason Wheat needed that child. Whatever the need might be, Hank intended to make sure that it kept Packy safe until this emergency was over. Then he'd see what he could do to get him back to Momma Grace.

Chapter 15

When Mel Bergen arrived at the clubhouse shortly after noon, Sanchez noticed that his usual air of self-importance had vanished. Roger Martineau's body had been removed to the morgue, but there was enough gruesome evidence of the murder on the cool deck to leave the mayor ashen-faced. He tiptoed around like a man treading barefoot on splinters of glass. He seemed to be questioning some of his attitudes. Hank thought it might do him a world of good.

"The people on that mountain could just as well have turned their anger on me," Bergen muttered and gave a shudder. "They may have assumed that I wasn't taking their problems seriously. And of course, that's far from the truth. The town's been discussing all kinds of plans for their relief."

He appeared to be somewhat reassured by Detective Lubeck's firm handshake and matter-of-fact explanation of the work being done by the technicians.

"Do you have a suspect?" Bergen blinked at the fresh graffiti on the wall. "That looks like gibberish to me."

"We'll have a better idea when we get this data processed," Lubeck told him. "Couple of days, at least, before we can make any statements."

When the tour ended, Sanchez walked the mayor back to his car. Mel grunted as he squeezed under the steering wheel and fumbled for the seat belt. "I believe I'll write a personal letter to each family on

Spanish Saddle Mountain. You know, to convince them of our continued support and concern for their problems. Let them know how determined we are to solve this matter, to keep the water flowing. Mary Anne can get them in the mail today." He slumped against the leather upholstery, hands gripping the steering wheel, knuckles white.

"Is there a plan to get water up the mountain?" Sanchez asked. It was the first mention he'd heard of any solutions.

Bergen stiffened. "Well, there's always a solution," he huffed. "I'm speaking generally, of course. Our citizens deserve our very best time and attention on this matter. With the council's help…" He ran out of breath and stared into space, looking dejected. "We'll have to cancel the festival."

Hank leaned on the open door. He knew Pella had been sending out advance publicity for months. "There isn't time to get the word out, Mel. The rodeo and craft people are due tomorrow. Some may already be on the road. You want to send back all those entrance fees?" He scowled at the open space beyond the road where the fireworks display was scheduled to blast off on Saturday night. "But we could cancel the pyrotechnics."

"Not on your life." Some color was creeping back into the mayor's face. "We aren't going do that to Ford Wheat." He straightened his spine, squirmed in his seat and cleared his throat. "Uh…Do you think it might be a smart idea to bring Bud Brickson in on the council's water committee?"

Much to the annoyance of Greenwood Development, the fifty resident families, the Chuparrosa people who owned golfing privileges and realtors promoting the lots, the entire sports complex at Sonoran Skyline was off limits to all but the police for two days. Luanne and her son packed their bags and went off to stay with relatives in Tucson.

Marshal Sanchez and his deputies engaged in a bit of casual questioning in Chuparrosa and found that attitudes about the murder were mixed. No one claimed Martineau deserved his violent end, but most agreed that he had displayed a knuckle-headed skill for irritating a good share of the community, particularly non-golfers who couldn't afford a home costing several million. And he had grossly underestimated the antagonism of the thirsty homeowners on Spanish Saddle Mountain.

Then there was the matter of the petroglyphs. If Martineau had sold them as artifacts to the highest bidder, the state might have stepped in. Instead, Roger had used his excellent business sense and total disregard for ancient mysteries by putting the stones on display in the new Sacred Stones Clubhouse. A return to *in situ* preservation was the only arrangement that would satisfy the outraged members of the Archaeology Club. Many in town were in sympathy with them. But who in Chuparrosa would kill a man because he just doesn't get it?

Late on Wednesday afternoon, Sanchez had once again taken time to drive out to Agatha's adobe shack. This time he noticed that the pale round rocks in the creek displayed four inches of crusty white rings above the current water level, a sure sign that the water table in the stream was falling.

He'd found her standing in her garden, waist deep in tepary bean vines. A burden basket half full of bean pods rested on her back. As usual the calm, innocent smile bloomed among the wrinkles on her face. She refused to talk until he followed her up the cactus-lined path to sit cross-legged in the shade of the mesquite tree with a cup of *atole*.

"You've come about Mr. Martineau's passing to the spirit world," Agatha murmured. She reached for the burden basket full of beans and began to pop open the leathery shells, letting the white stream chatter through her fingers into a bowl.

"Who brought you the news?" Few people ventured onto the single dirt track unless Agatha's hut was their destination.

"Two nights ago I saw it in a dream." She closed her eyes as if giving the vision an instant replay.

"Did you see the reason for his death?"

"He destroyed the shrine. He took the life stone, which protected him as well."

"Come on, Agatha. He just put them back together in another place." Sanchez knew she wouldn't go for that explanation. He didn't believe in it either.

"The house they are building for the stones is not sacred. It will be destroyed."

Hank swallowed some of the *atole*, sweet with corn meal and fragrant with cinnamon. It didn't help him bridge the gap between his world and the one Agatha inhabited. "We think Roger Martineau was murdered. Do you know who could've killed him?"

"Of course." Her smile was patient, pitying. "The one the gods appointed for the task."

"His name?" he asked, doubting her answer would help.

She paused in her shelling to tip up her cup, swallow the last of the *atole* and wipe a hand across her mouth. *"I'char tontha,"* she said, speaking in her created Hohokam language. "The gods' appointed."

"It won't do me any good to run that through the computer, Agatha. I have to have his real name. Is it Isaiah?"

She got to her feet, picked up the empty cups and began to walk to her house. The audience was over. Before she reached the door, she turned. "There is good news. The stones will be replaced very soon now." Then she bent and disappeared through the low T-shaped doorway.

After dark that evening, as the marshal drove out between Sonoran Skyline's tall gate pillars, he noticed Bud Brickson standing on the roadside. Caught in the patrol car's headlights, the man looked gaunt and ghostlike. He waved his arms to attract the marshal's attention

"I walked down the mountain in hopes of catching you," Bud said when Hank had pulled off Buckskin Road and beckoned him into the patrol car. He was trembling, his hands clutching each other, fingers lacing and unlacing. He took three deep breaths before he spoke again in a voice ragged with emotion. "Marshal, what did we have to do with this tragedy?"

"Damned if I know, Bud," Hank said. He understood that "we" meant the people on Spanish Saddle Mountain. "It's way too soon in the investigation to start assigning blame."

"We were simply trying to hang on to our lifestyle, honestly and legally. Our share of a disappearing resource." His voice rose in pitch until it was a shrill whine. "Did that lead someone to murder Martineau?"

"Who do you suspect?"

Bud stared at the marshal, head shaking, despair in his pale eyes. His mouth opened and closed several times before he clamped it shut and turned away. "None of our people. We were in agreement about doing this by the book."

"Does Isaiah Morley operate by that book?"

Bud's face registered a puzzled half-attention as he swiveled to look at Hank. "Who? No, no, those boys are Jeremiah and Micah. They talk wild and dumb, but Sugar promised to keep them in line." He stared down at his writhing hands, grabbing at them to hold them still. "The Morleys are the most likely to lose everything. It's always been a bare bones business up there, but now that they have to haul in water...The place is mortgaged. None of our homes have any value without water."

Sanchez nosed his car back onto the road. He'd put in a fifteen-hour day, and he felt tired as hell. "I'll drive you home," he said.

Up the hill he sent Bud tottering toward his door and continued on the mountain road, turning in at the long driveway that led to Fiesta's place. To the southwest he could see St. Jude's Thumb, a slim, black barricade looming against the lights of the Valley. Night and distance blocked out the gray shroud of pollution and city blight so plain in the daytime. The cities and towns below sparkled with seductive promise.

Fiesta laughed when she saw him standing at her door, a knowing, intimate laugh, churned up from somewhere deep within herself. She led him toward the overstuffed cushions of her living room. *"Bienvenida."*

He was too tired for her games, too conscious of his hunger and rumpled appearance. "Speak English," he ordered. "This is business."

"Si senor. It's always business. Would you prefer cerveza or a glass of wine?"

He shook his head, but she brought him a Dos XX anyway, poured into a frosty mug from the freezer behind her bar. He lowered himself onto her curved sofa, watching as she shucked her sandals and curled up beside him with a glass of Zinfandel the color of her tank top. Her dark hair was confined in a braid long enough to hang over one shoulder. A turquoise ribbon, tucked into the end, bobbed just above her left breast.

"A toast to Roger Martineau." Fiesta raised her glass with a cynical grin. "May his specter forever haunt the dry and deserted fairways of Sonoran Skyline."

Sanchez shrugged and drank deeply from the mug. Play along, he thought, in case she knows something useful. "Bud's decided to stop the picketing."

"Bud is an antique gnome with no guts. He may embrace the guilt for Roger's death, but the rest of us do not. My friends from the media will be out on Friday and there'll be a flock of us down there to greet 'em." She stretched out her arm to trace the shape of Hank's ear with one finger, her voice as caressing as the desert breeze. "You come too, *cariño.*"

Sanchez twisted to face her, putting his ear beyond her reach. "Who's coming?"

"At least twenty. Four Morleys, of course, Zephyr Wilson, and that Neanderthal she lives with. Some others. And Louise promised a big delegation from the archaeology club. They're all mad as hell about the shrine in the clubhouse."

"Not five Morleys? Not Isaiah?"

A slow smile lifted the corners of her mouth. "Did you know we've filed a law suit against Greenwood Development?" she asked. "With that and the media coverage, we may be able to get their attention."

"You'd be smarter to work on the mayor and the council. They're afraid of being the next victims."

She gave him another hot blast of her alluring smile. It promised a long and loving night. Sanchez sat up straighter. "You're not going to help me with this, are you?"

The bright ribbon bobbed up and down as Fiesta shook her head.

He tossed off the last of his beer and got to his feet. Except for the view at the other end of the sofa and the badly needed refreshment, coming here had been a waste of his time. "You'll be associating with a killer."

"Would you care?"

"Fiesta, this guy is dangerous. I don't want any of my friends hanging around with him."

She sat staring at him, bare arms spread wide along the back of the sofa, her expression sulky. "Did you ever kill anyone, Marshal?"

"Once." He frowned. The scar from a bullet that had creased his eyebrow began to tingle. He willed himself not to rub it. "In the line of duty. To save my partner's life."

"What's worth saving from destruction? A life? A family? A lifestyle? Thirty six hundred acres of untouched desert? None of them can be replaced." Fiesta uncoiled her legs and rose, facing him, so close that he could smell her fragrance and see a pulse beating in her throat. "What would you kill for the next time? That anemic little blond of yours?"

Fiesta took his arm, marched him into the foyer and flung open the door. Then she stretched up against him, her mouth, her body, hard and angry, colliding with his, an attack not a kiss. "I think killers are adorable," she breathed, shoving him out onto the step. Before he could blurt out a retort, she slammed the heavy door behind him, leaving him in the darkness of the desert night, furious and mystified.

Chapter 16

On Thursday, Sanchez spent all day at Sonoran Skyline with the sheriff's deputies, studying every facet of the operation. A few indistinct tracks had been found in patches of sand, boots that might belong to the perp. From those he helped to figure triangulations and draw maps, absorbing information, trying to put the pieces together.

All other activities had to be postponed. His appointment with Greenwood Development was rescheduled for Monday. The weight of the coming festival pressed darkly on his mind. He knew as sure as the Sonoran Skyline golf courses were going to be watered, that there would be trouble somewhere in Chuparrosa during the next two days. The terrorist wasn't likely to tell him what or when.

Hank had worked his share of violent deaths as a cop in Albuquerque, but those killings had been impulsive, the victim and perpetrator unknown to him – random shootings, gang member homicides, robberies or drug deals gone wrong, women beaten to death by enraged partners. He knew it was the same in every big city.

The split between golfers and Nature lovers in Chuparrosa had happened slowly. It could have been handled and healed. But someone was taking advantage of the problem for reasons still obscure. Until the perpetrator's goal had been achieved, the town was in for more trouble. Sanchez had gone over the list of fifty or so possible suspects a dozen times and found them all wanting. Each person lacked motivation, physical strength or ability.

Isaiah Morley was the closest thing to a suspect they had, and he couldn't be found. Seemed like a cowboy-cartoonist with aqua marine eyes and terrorist tendencies would be easy to spot. Plenty of caves and arroyos laced their way through the mountains beyond Sugar's place. Isaiah would know that wilderness from childhood wanderings and have the skills to survive in it. Technical research had turned up an old sample of the man's fingerprint. The county police had found nothing that matched it at any of the crime scenes. A nation-wide query located him in Idaho. His parole officer hadn't seen him for a couple weeks, but wasn't concerned.

Given the lack of information, Sanchez had argued against calling in the FBI until after the festival, and Lubeck reluctantly agreed to wait. But, without any fanfare, every law enforcement officer in four states had his eye peeled for a guy named Isaiah Morley, their "person of interest".

By the end of the on-site investigation, Hank was dragging with weariness and no closer to a solution for any of the crimes. Agatha had insisted that Roger's death was an act of revenge by her own private gods. Bud assumed the guilt for himself and the water committee. Fiesta pretended it was justifiable homicide. The mayor, fearing that he might be next on the hit list, crept like a shadow in and out of his office at city hall.

And then there was the puzzle of Milford Wheat, his fireworks and his grandson. The memory of Packy's tears and the fragile arm that had tightened around Hank's neck continued to gnaw at him. Most kids told lies, but the boy's distress seemed real. Who was this Izzy who had been sent to fetch him from New York? The marshal had made a quick call to Elena Salado at her home before she left for work on Thursday, but Packy seemed to be a mystery to her as well.

"El es bueno niño, Mariscal. Muy bueno, pobre muchacho," she told him, in her musical Spanish. "So quiet and so shy. Not very happy. He eats like he's starving."

"Does he ever talk about his mother or where he lived in New York?" Hank asked.

"No, but he hardly ever talks. Mr. Wheat has a tutor come in every morning. I watch him in the afternoon, then give him his supper and get him to bed." She paused. "My English is not so good, you know. Packy has no Spanish."

Things sounded okay. Hank made some notes and chewed the end of his pencil. "Do you ever see any…ah…bruises?"

"Oh, no. His grandfather never lets him play outside. He says he's sickly. He did sneeze yesterday. But I don't know…"

A look in a child's eyes wasn't enough to build a hunch on. He was wasting his time. "*Gracias,* Elena. Let me know if you see anything strange or if Packy gets hurt."

"There is one strange thing, though," Elena said. "All his clothes have tags."

"With his name?" Even Packy/Josef seemed confused about his name.

"No, I mean store tags. Every stitch he owns is new."

When he left Sonoran Skyline late Thursday afternoon, Marshal Sanchez hesitated and then pointed the nose of his pickup north on Buckskin Road, heading for the national forest, an enormous area of public land that sprawled around Chuparrosa on the east and north. He'd been mulling over this trek into the wilderness all day, convinced it was a fool's errand, but between the hunches and tidbits of information, he'd been gripped by the urge to make at least a token search for Isaiah Morley.

Could he be the man in the photo with sunglasses, the one who tried to kidnap Pella, killed Martineau and drowned his dog, all the time quoting Bible verses? The cops were still scratching their heads over the graffiti, but Hank had checked with the Chuparrosa Library once again, and this time, shared the code with Lubeck. The new reference from Isaiah, on the Sonoran Skyline Clubhouse wall, had been read over the phone to him in a breathless voice by Janet Peterson. "It promises rivers in the desert, water to a chosen people," she said. "And most interesting of all, to the wild beasts, as well. A fine ecological statement, I think." Well, it left no doubt about this Isaiah's purpose. Had the man also warmed the heart of Agnes Pure Stone?

No one had seen him. The Morleys could be expected to form a line of solidarity and lie, rather than admit his location. He could be holed up somewhere, a place where he could sit out a manhunt and not attract attention. Hank knew of springs in the forest that dripped water year round and caves that could provide shelter if you weren't too fussy about the accommodations. A boy growing up on Spanish Saddle Mountain would have a map of them in his mind.

The forest in the Sonoran Desert wasn't a forest in the familiar sense of tall pines. It was rugged country, piles of granite boulders and sand, well covered with chaparral, administrated by the Forest Service as a watershed for the big cities in the valley and grazing leases for the cattle ranchers. On the far side of Spanish Saddle Mountain, less than a twenty-minute hike from Sugar's back door, lay the forest boundary. Beyond were rocky slopes sprinkled with creosote bush, burrsage and cat claw. Access to this wilderness from Buckskin Road was by a rutted trail called Forest Road 13. A popular groomed road, F.R.14, six miles beyond, bore most of the traffic into the forest from the south. It led to gentle hiking in dry arroyos and a popular fishing stream. If Isaiah wanted solitude, Hank figured he could travel overland from Morleys' and find it in the lonesome wilderness off F.R.13.

The clock in the pickup showed five-fifteen when the marshal bounced his truck onto the unimproved track that was better for hiking than driving. Too late in the day for more than just a cursory look around. If he found anything promising, he'd have to call Lubeck and his guys back for the search. He pulled to a stop under a mesquite tree and stepped out. To his right Spanish Saddle Mountain rose another five hundred feet to its pinnacle. Fiesta's home lay snuggled up there with a view of both Chuparrosa and the northern mountains. Directly behind him, but farther down, stood the Morley property. Between the two places, erosion had scooped the saddle that gave the mountain its name. From the back side, where he stood, neither home could be seen.

Sanchez squinted at the loose sand on the surface of the road. The brief shower of a week ago had left it pock-marked, but he sorted out four sets of tire tracks that had been made later. And they all looked the same. Had one vehicle been roaming up and down this isolated way?

He walked east, following the tire tracks, watching for a landmark he'd noticed during an exploratory hike months before. He hoped no one had made off with it. The low afternoon sun seared his back, and he felt no cooling in the humid little breeze that had gathered the swarm of gnats whining in his ears. Cumulus clouds high over the mountains signaled a welcome chance of more rain. He stumped along the ridge for half a mile before he found the cactus that marked the way down – a ten-foot tall saguaro, topped by a rare mutation called a crown. The tracks stopped, as well, and some activity had disturbed more of the sand.

From here a narrow old foot trail wound around the shrubs and scrubby trees and down the slippery hillside into the canyon. Stones of all sizes littered the ground, creating ball bearings for careless feet. Hank kept well away from the curved thorns of the cat claws that thrived in the place. He searched as he descended, eyes on the ground, but there seemed to be no sign of footprints or litter that would have signaled frequent use. Except for bird song, the only sounds came from the occasional rattle of a pickup on distant Buckskin Road.

Both vegetation and gnats thickened as Sanchez neared the bottom of the canyon. Deep-rooted cottonwood and sycamore trees grew tall on water runoff from the hills above, but the springtime plants in the wash were now a crisp brown. The place smelled of sun-dried summer. Sanchez stepped into the knee-high growth at the foot of the slope and moved cautiously upstream, his eyes studying the bank. The coolness of vegetation flowed up to him, but details were hard to see in the canyon's deep shade. He paused and scanned the area for signs of habitation, listening for sounds of rustling. High overhead a zone-tailed hawk swooped up, screaming objections to his presence in the canyon. Good, Hank thought, hoping it meant no one else was around. He took another swipe at the gnats and moved on.

He slogged through the undergrowth for another two hundred feet, adding to the collection of weed seeds clinging to his pants, and came to a halt at a low stone cliff. The uneven granite bedrock was streaked with white lines running down in vertical stripes. He ran his hand over them, feeling the delicate ridges of minerals built up over hundreds of years. The tiny spring he'd found last winter no longer seeped a steady trickle of moisture. The water that fed generations of sycamores in this lush canyon had dried up. Would another wildlife habitat soon be lost thanks to Sonoran Skyline?

A few steps more brought him to the cave, set above the wash on a ledge of rock, high enough to be safe from a sudden flood. The remote location also had a spectacular view of the distant mountains and, formerly, running water. The primitive shelter appealed to Hank as a camping spot. It could be even more attractive to a man on the run.

He pulled out his flashlight, scrambled up the bank to the foot-wide ledge.

The cave opening was a ten-foot yawn in the side of the slope and the interior depth measured the same. Rough sides and floor of stone had been hollowed out by Nature over centuries, as floods swept down this minor canyon. A bedroll could be tossed on the floor for sleeping, with room left for a storage of some sort. Lacking water, Isaiah could have carried jugs of it from his parents house, hiked down from F.R. 13 and hidden what he needed where no one would find it. Not exactly fancy, Hank thought, but for temporary housing, it would do. He ran the beam of his flashlight around the space, into the farthest crannies, the arched ceiling, looking for any scrap of trash, evidence of habitation. But there was nothing. Even the pebbles, sticks and animal droppings that always collect in caves, had been swept out, probably into the wash. Strange. It had been picked too clean. If Isaiah had been here in the last few days, why had he left?

Something small and black scuttled slowly across the stone floor to join its buddies in a shallow cavity. Hank stared and let his light sweep the walls again. Conenose beetles, he thought, dozens of them. Brushed out, they'd come right back. No one with knowledge of the desert would risk bedding down with those sluggish bloodsuckers. Isaiah had been in that cave, he felt sure, and now he was gone. Did that mean the man's acts of terror were almost over?

Feeling cheated, he glanced at his watch. Almost seven and getting dark. The zone-tailed hawk rose from his perch in a sycamore and soared over the wash once more, his scream a warning. Sanchez moved back onto the path to begin the upward climb. A careful man, Isaiah Morley, he mused, a man who leaves no fingerprints, no trail. They would have to meet before this could be over. His greatest concern was that, when they finally did, it would not be on Isaiah's terms.

Chapter 17

A quick phone call to Pella as soon as he turned back onto Buckskin Road cemented Hank's plans for dinner, but it was eight-thirty before she could break away from the last flurry of festival details and come with him to the Miner's Delight Saloon. In one of the back booths, buffered from the general merriment, they ordered barbecued ribs and mugs of beer.

Tonight Charlie's place swarmed with customers. Men and women in jeans and Stetsons crowded the length of the mahogany bar swapping stories as they downed beer, whiskey and margaritas. The brass rail that paralleled the lower edge of the bar disappeared under a stampede of cowboy boots. A Western trio on the corner stage bellowed their vigorous laments, but the sound was swallowed up in the clamor of voices and shrieks of laughter. By the time their plates arrived, Charlie Talaferro joined them, squeezing in beside Hank, looking across the table with obvious pleasure at Pella in blue jeans and striped jersey.

"The rodeo crowd's found us," he said waggling his head toward the bar. "As many of 'em as can squeeze in anyway, plus their families and hands. Some had to go to the Jimson Weed and the Coyote Coral, I guess." Charlie smoothed his mustache and laughed. "I spent the whole afternoon with your lady out at the arena gettin' everybody set up for the first rounds tomorrow. Now they're gonna kick back 'n party. So what's new with the murder?"

Hank shook his head. "After two days we know when and how, but not who and why." He filled his mouth with the best slaw in Chuparrosa, wondering how to tell Charlie to go away without offending him.

"I thought 'why' was the fight over water," he persisted. "According to Jerry Morley, people on the Mountain feel they've won the battle."

"But not the war. Do they think Greenwood Development is going to let their fairways die as a memorial to Roger Martineau? They won't stop watering until the courts force them to stop." Hank put down a rib and wiped his hands. "How did the Morleys come to name their boys after Old Testament prophets?"

Charlie shrugged. "That's way before my time. I've heard they were involved in some hellfire and brimstone church back then. Jerry told me once that his dad got drummed out of the congregation for drinkin' beer and swearin' at the preacher when he came around for contributions. Ol' Jer seemed pretty proud of that." He gave a sputtering chuckle. "Sugar kept up her membership for awhile. She wanted the boys to get all that preachin', so she took them until they were old enough to want to stay home with their dad. Guess the holy names couldn't compete with Butch's good-ole-boy lessons."

He pushed himself to the end of the bench and stood up. "You two takin' good care of each other?" he asked.

Pella wiped some of the goo off her hands with the damp red towel that came with the ribs. "We're both taking care of me, Charlie. Hank doesn't need anything."

Sanchez felt Charlie's curious glance dart between them. "Um... Well, enjoy your dinner. The apple cobbler's prime tonight. I'll send some over." He turned away, heading for the folks at the bar, greeting customers on all sides.

Hank studied the top of Pella's golden head as she bent over her plate. She'd been preoccupied since Roger Martineau's murder. Who could blame her? The wound of her husband's tragic death two years before would never completely heal. Six months ago, after her friend Amelia Cuthbert had died a violent death, she'd wanted to run, to escape the memories. He'd needed all his powers of persuasion to talk her into staying in Chuparrosa. Now he wondered if it might have been easier on both of them if she'd ignored him and moved to San Diego. Much as he loved her, he wasn't prepared to make this one-sided romance his life's work.

She looked up and met his eyes. "Hank, when will your deputies stop trailing me around? That creep hasn't left calls on my answering machine since the attack at the high school. He's not interested in me anymore."

"We might have had him if we'd started following you earlier." He could lose her as easily by smothering her with protection as by withdrawing it. "What's your hurry?"

"I've got job interviews lined up all next week."

"Daytime? Where?"

"La Estrella Shopping Center in Scottsdale, a couple of computer companies. A temp agency. Even the Chuparrosa Museum." She grinned and picked up her beer mug. "Be happy for me, Hank. I might at last be paid a living wage."

"I don't think he'll follow you to the Valley. You'll keep wearing the security lavaliere?"

"It's a permanent part of my wardrobe." She made a face at him. "I see it as a modern version of the chastity belt. If anybody lays a hand on Pella, she explodes his eardrums."

"I've noticed your chastity is pretty well protected without it," he growled. "It's your life I'm concerned about."

Pella ducked her head and began scrubbing her hands with the towel. "Yes, and I need to get on with it. I've got to have a job, Hank."

"Any of those businesses would be damn lucky to have you." He knew what might be coming in the next two days, and tonight his feelings were close to the surface. "Here's to your future, *querida.*" He picked up her hand and touched his lips to her sticky palm. It seemed less and less likely that he would ever say "and ours."

Chapter 18

The marshal stood in the wings of the high school auditorium, trying to keep cool amid the bodies stuffed into the limited back stage space. From this cramped vantage point, he had watched the festival pageant unfold. Now, just after intermission, Fiesta Flores and her partner were pounding the stage in an emotionally charged flamenco dance. Close, without touching, the man pressed toward her, predatory arms raised, smoldering eyes caressing her, while Fiesta, the flounces on her polka-dot dress held high, back arched, breasts jutting, swished and spun on her black shoes. It was a performance calculated to raise the blood pressure of every adult and teenager in the audience. Bursts of clapping and shouts hurled in excited Spanish challenged the dancers to greater heights of interpretation.

In front of Hank, the column of little girls in his charge had stopped giggling and pinching each other, their attention all at once riveted by this new awareness of sensuality. Disguised as palo verde trees in pale green tights and yellow tulle, the children were sandwiched between Pella at the stage end and Hank at the back. Beside them Tyler and the two Morley boys supported the desert scenery that would be run onto the stage as soon as the curtain fell on Fiesta's dance.

Nearby Maud Florence in her pale blue muumuu and Reeboks, white hair drifting out of its ponytail, let out a groan of despair as the tight spot light she had demanded for the flamenco, zigged when the dancers zagged, and for an instant, the pair vanished into upstage darkness.

With intermission over at the opening night's pageant performance, the show had settled down, more or less, to a working production. Children from previous and future acts were confined to the dressing rooms, where they were being entertained by indulgent parents. So except for Maud Florence, the off-stage area was calm.

"Poor Maud. She's wired tonight," Pella had murmured earlier as they'd watched her giving final instructions and shuffling the notes that sifted through her stiff fingers onto the floor. Hank gathered them up and handed them back, knowing she'd never get them in order again.

Thanks to Bent, who was stage manager, the show had gone on with only a few minor hitches. Two children in saguaro suits were treated for bumped heads when they collided on their dash to the restroom. The caps for the cowboys' pistols disappeared at the last moment, and the kids had to shout "Bang, Bang" as they brandished them at the end of their song. When a dozen four-year-olds, dressed as cactus wrens, were led onstage, a couple of them, much to their parents' and grandparents' tittering delight, sucked their fingers in pigeon-toed awe instead of singing their song.

Six more acts and then the finale.

The palo verde trees came out of their trance like windup toys when Fiesta, her partner and guitarist began bowing to wild applause. The curtain was dropped. The scenery changers jogged onstage, followed by the squirming children and director Maud.

"We've got this aced," Pella crowed as she and Hank ran into the bowels of the gym to collect the next act. They herded six small boys, garbed as early gold miners, into the wings, lined them up and shushed them.

Hank was attempting to keep the wiggly miners from tearing off their false mustaches, when Fiesta swirled by. She hesitated and then leaned close, holding the ruffles of her skirt to her waist with one hand. With the other she pulled his head down to whisper in his ear.

"You've got to do something about Zephyr Wilson."

He shot a quick glance over the miner's bobbing heads and stretched for a troublemaker's shoulder in time to stop a punch. Pella, half-lit by the bright lights of the stage, was staring at Fiesta with a look of puzzlement that blossomed into revelation.

"Why?" he asked. "What's going on?"

"Jake Scarlett's going to kill her."

"What's different about tonight? He's been trying to do that for months. She won't file a complaint."

Fiesta glanced away for a moment. "You don't have to know why. He's just a beast. And this time he is going to kill her." She shifted her weight toward him, her ruffles foaming around his legs. "Can you protect her?"

He pulled a cell phone from his pocket and began to push buttons. "I'll send Rhys Jones out to their place right away. But she's got to get out and stay out. Talk to her, Fiesta. Make her listen."

She nodded, looking dissatisfied. "Is that the little glacier you're in love with?" Her dark head tipped in Pella's direction. "She is a child, *amante*. You deserve much more."

The palo verde trees were lingering over their bows. Hank spoke a few urgent words into the phone and tapped it off, before he grasped Fiesta's elbows, steadying her as he moved aside and began to hand the small miners their shovels.

"You always put on a flawless performance, Fiesta. Your audience adores you," he said.

She swept her skirts away from him, elegant head held high and started for the dressing rooms. "But you, *señor*, are a bitter disappointment."

The grand finale ended the pageant with all the performers on stage, including Maud who was given a huge bouquet of yellow roses and a standing ovation that painted her cheeks pink with pleasure.

Half an hour later the scenery had been stacked and the costumes hung up. Hank strolled with Pella through the nearly empty parking lot to his pickup. The last of the adult cast members and stage crew were ducking out the rear door, hollering wisecracks to each other, their arms full of equipment and props, their thoughts on plans to meet at the

Miners' Delight for beers and a cool down after the strenuous performance. The stillness of the evening was shattered by the clang of pickup trucks being loaded, car doors slamming shut and the roar of motors. One by one, they pulled onto the gravel drive that curved toward the main road to town.

"I want to stop at Sonoran Skyline for a couple minutes to check on Kevin," Hank said. "He's moonlighting tonight as a guard at the club house construction site."

"Will you take me home then?" Pella asked.

"Sure." He'd run up to Zephyr Wilson's place after that and try to have a word with Jake Scarlett. Rhys had found no one home earlier in the evening and had checked out all the bars before going back to stake out the house. So far neither Jake nor Zephyr had returned. When they did show up, the marshal was going to plant himself at their rundown house until Zephyr filed a complaint against Scarlett and moved to the Cactus Blossom Motel for the night. Either way, it meant a few more hours on the job. He grinned down at Pella. "Big day tomorrow. I've got to be out early lining up the parade, so I'll pick you up before six-thirty."

He slung his arm over her shoulders. She didn't draw away, but seemed to be only tolerating his closeness, not sharing it. He moved his hand to the back of her neck, stroking it gently.

"Don't," she said, and tossed her head, the blond cap of hair flipping out in a halo, shiny in the glare of headlights.

They reached the truck, parked beneath one of the light poles. Hank unlocked the right hand door and watched her jump in, her high-heeled sandals clicking on the step of the cab, the short silky skirt of her dress swaying around bare legs, her eyes looking anywhere but at him.

"I appreciated your help tonight," she said after he'd started the motor. "Tomorrow night's crew should be able to handle things without us."

"You're turning me loose?"

"It'll be a long day. Duty at the parade at 6:30. Then there's the old settlers' picnic at noon, another day of the craft show, rodeo and band concert, plus the fireworks display after the pageant. Mr. Wheat's going to be overseeing that, but I'll have to be there, too. Will you be checking the crowd or the fireworks?"

Fireworks. In the marshal's mind it contained all the menace of an old west shoot out. Sometime during the evening it would become a test of wills between him and the slender man with powerful arms, who couldn't wait for a chance to cause more destruction. He didn't want Pella there at all, but he had no power to chase her away.

"*Querida*, I'm hangin' out with you until we catch this guy. You've cast yourself as bait while the festival is on, so you're the best chance we have to snag him. Wherever you go, I go, *amiga mia.*" The flip reply was meant to save her pride, to pretend the marshal's office needed her more than she needed protection.

He slammed the pickup into gear and turned onto the street that led to Sonoran Skyline. There were times when her Anglo-Saxon stoicism made him want to shake her. His ex-wife's bouts of hysterics had been tough to deal with, but he wished Pella would scream at him once in a while, just to show she cared.

He'd been unable to spare a deputy to run after her during the first day of the festival, and Charlie was busy at the rodeo, so Tyler Bent took over the job. From the reports Sanchez got, Pella had kept Bent moving, as she checked on her chair people from the center of town, where the craft show had blossomed to the tunes of the oompah band, to the arena a couple miles to the west where calf roping and barrel racing raised the dust and enchanted the fans. Fortunately, there was less risk in the daylight in spite of the big crowds they were drawing. Bent had made a point of telling Hank what a great time they'd had. He was planning to do it again on Saturday.

"How long have you known Fiesta Flores?" Pella asked, an innocent question out of the blue.

Hank pulled up at the stop sign behind a line of other trucks, alert to the change of subject. "I met her when I came to Chuparrosa."

"She's gorgeous, isn't she? A fantastic dancer. The two of you together...um...you looked like two characters in the same story. Like you touched each other in a hundred ancient ways."

He gunned the pickup around the corner. "Okay. I guess that's reasonable. We're both Hispanic, both from New Mexico. Fiesta's…easy for a man to get to know."

"But you have a rapport that goes beyond acquaintance." Regret wavered in her voice. "Were you lovers? Are you lovers?"

Hank laughed and turned to look at her. "I'm just a country boy, *querida.* One woman at a time is all I can handle."

The lights on the Sonoran Skyline gatehouse shone ahead. On an impulse he guided the pickup into a bare spot across the road, avoiding the water committee's picket signs, and put his foot on the brake. She wanted to talk? Well, he wanted to talk.

"What did you mean last night when you told Charlie I didn't need anything?"

Pella shrugged her shoulders. "You're completely self-sufficient. Calm, patient, in control. Everything a cop is supposed to be." The sadness remained in her voice. "You manage your life without help from anyone."

There'd been a time when that answer would have pleased him. Hearing it from her now made him mad. "You know damn well what I need," he exploded. "I'm going nuts waiting for you to bury your husband."

Her head jerked away as if he'd hit her. She hit back. "I've heard how macho Hispanic men are," she shouted. "You probably beat your women!"

Good! he thought. A little warmth, a little fire. Hell, was she challenging him to force her? He remembered Zephyr Wilson and all the other battered women he'd seen in his years as a cop. "Not this Hispanic, *nena.* We're together tonight because I have to be with you. I need your ideas, your smiles, your softness, your caring. I need your love."

Hank reached for her, wanting to breathe those words into her ear in Spanish, but Pella smoldered, staring out into the darkness. He let the brake off with an oath and spun the truck across the road into the gatehouse drive.

"'Evening, Russ," he said to the uniformed man who stepped to the door. "We're going in to check on Kevin. Any problems tonight?"

The man peered into the car, one hand on the sill of the truck's open window as if to prevent them from moving on, his slicked-down hair reflecting the overhead lights.

"Things is as quiet as a dead cell phone." He chuckled, showing tobacco-stained teeth, and raised two fingers in a salute to Pella. "If you'll excuse the expression, ma'am. All fifty sets of residents are tucked into their homes long since. Scared, they are. Four of 'em have put their houses up for sale now, and the others are talkin' about it. They didn't even go to the pageant."

Hank nodded and started to ease the truck forward.

Russ's grin grew broader. "My granddaughter's one of them palo verde trees, ya' know," he announced, leaning his arms on the window and breathing pepperoni into Hank's face. "They wear these li'l green costumes and dance around. She's in quite a dither about it. My wife and I are goin' tomorrow night."

"It's a great show," Sanchez agreed, letting the engine gradually pull the man's arms out of the window. "One more stop and then we're for home. 'Night, Russ."

They drove the curving street that wound past the office, skirting the widely separated houses off to the south. The streetlights were subdued, but the glow made the blackness outside their spheres more intense. Lights from one of the Sonoran Skyline patrol cars could be seen crawling over the road that crossed Rifleman Mesa. The golf courses lay deep in an obsidian void. In the western sky, a thumbnail moon rocked on Cloud Builder Mountain.

The pickup bumped along the makeshift road toward the clubhouse, past dim shapes of saguaros and mesquite trees in wooden crates lining the track. Hank swerved to avoid a snarl of metal strapping and nosed to a stop beside Kevin's pickup.

"Come with me," he coaxed Pella. He knew she was still mad at him, but for some reason the outside construction lights were turned off. He couldn't leave her here alone, and he didn't want an argument. "Ol' Kevin'll appreciate a break in the boredom."

They had to concentrate in order to walk up the rough driveway following a flashlight beam. Stepping over stones, around bags of cement, pallets and debris, Sanchez held his hand under Pella's elbow to keep her from stumbling. There was no light coming from the structure looming before them. It stood like a ruin, one shade blacker than the blackness of the sky, blocking off the stars, walls uneven with a massive spider web of scaffolding showing above. The adulterated air held the choking smell of lumber and cement dust.

A sudden, uneasy instinct made Sanchez pull Pella to a halt. He put an arm around her. "Something's wrong," he muttered and raised his head, listening for a sound he hadn't quite heard, only sensed. He whispered again. "Kevin should have been out here to see who we were." He shut off the flashlight and tried to make his eyes pierce the gloom. There was a wave of shadow. No, two. Then the shadows became silhouetted figures, slender, agile, scampering away from the building.

In an instant, Hank twirled Pella to the sand and dropped on top of her. His hands covered her face, as the ground shook with an explosion that turned the sky to fire and smothered them with sifting dust. Pellets of rock and litter stung Hank's back. He felt Pella gasp and struggle beneath him and then lie still, as the impact of the blast shuddered through them.

"Stay here," he commanded, when the rocks stopped falling. He rolled off her body and crouched behind a frail screen of ocotillo, craning his neck to see without being seen. One faintly discernible figure paused on the crest of a nearby mound north of the clubhouse, its form lit by the flames from the burning scaffolding. All in black, the featureless imp danced for joy.

Fury brought a growl from Hank's throat. His deputy had been left for dead, crushed under a pile of rocks by a maniac. The figure turned to flee, and Hank burst into pursuit. He never carried a gun off-duty, but the runner wasn't that far away. If he caught the guy, he'd dismember him.

The figure paused for an instant. Then a blast of light came from the hillock. Hank heard a scream from Pella before the force of the bullet sent him sprawling on the gravel. He cursed himself for a fool. He had exposed them all to this eco-psychopath.

"Stay in the shadows! Don't move!" he yelled at Pella as soon as he could breathe. He struggled onto his back, sat up and then crouched, keeping low. The little hill was now bare of all shapes except the gaunt saguaros. The guy with the gun could be anywhere. Every rise in this rolling terrain offered shelter. Hank searched through the smoke for movement, one hand pressing the wound in his right shoulder. Nothing vital had been hit, he guessed. There was a lot of blood soaking his shirt, running down his arm. No pain, yet. With luck he could get to the demolished clubhouse and find his deputy before it started to hurt.

The ruined hulk of stone gave off a ragged glow that shimmered red in the dust from the explosion. Flames from the scaffold boards shot toward the sky. The building was mostly stone and mortar, but the fire could get hot enough to catch the treated beams supporting the heavy stone walls.

Sanchez scurried along the sheltering aisle of boxed trees, keeping low, until he reached the roughed-in front patio, now a tumble of boulders spewed out by the explosion, and began to creep across the space. Over the crackle of burning timbers, he heard the truck door slam and felt a surge of impotent fury. Why in hell wouldn't Pella follow orders just once? She couldn't go for help; he had the ignition key in his pocket. But not his cell phone, damn it. If the *pinché* bomber was still in the area, he could make his evening's performance complete by snatching Pella, too. Or shooting her dead.

He paused in the shadow of one of the gigantic columns erected as a future support for the structure's roof and peered back along the path to where the light from the fire was reflected in the chrome of the two pickups. There was no question of his returning to the truck before he'd found Kevin. He'd have to pray that she'd lock the doors and keep out of sight.

He turned back toward the cavernous building, feeling the hellish heat of the fire on his face. Burning boards and beams illuminated the upper portions of the vast entrance hall, from time to time dropping pieces to the ground in a shower of sparks that revealed the extent of the damage. The reinforced concrete columns had survived the blast, but much of the stone facing lay on the cracked slab. The bomb itself, he guessed, had been located in the great chimney. There was nothing left of that wall but ridges of twisted metal. The huge shrine rocks he had seen being placed above the mantle piece now littered the floor.

He took a deep breath and plunged into the smoky ruin, climbing over the pile of debris, sweeping it with his flashlight. He braced himself for the possibility that he might find his deputy crushed under this avalanche. His boot caught in a crevice. He yanked it loose, rolling across the next boulder to an exposed portion of the slab where he could shine a light on the stones from other angles. He felt a wave of relief. No signs of a body could be seen between the piles of rubble.

Sanchez was beginning to pant. His right arm felt cold. "Kevin," he yelled and pointed his flashlight beam into other crannies. Dust swirled through the light, bleaching out the colors to one drab tone. He didn't know what Kevin was wearing. Jeans or khaki, probably. Equally invisible in the dust and smoke.

A low groan reached him, and at the same time, he became aware of the distant sound of sirens. Russ must have called them, he thought with a grim smile and swiveled the light in direction of the sound.

Kevin lay on his side in an alcove, a trussed-up heap, his hands and feet tied together behind his back. A gag of cloth stretched his mouth. Blood from a gash on his head reddened his sandy hair and ran into his eyes. The shelter of the alcove had protected him from the worst of the rockfall, *gracias a Dios,* but two of the flaming boards from the scaffolding lay across his legs, burning away his jeans.

Sanchez kicked the timbers off Kevin's body and sank to the floor beside him, using his left hand to pat out the fire that was roasting the man's clothing and flesh. He felt himself growing weaker and fought to keep from passing out. With his knife, he cut out the gag and began sawing the ropes. His deputy was moaning, unconscious. His own shoulder began to throb in regular painful bursts.

The noise of the sirens intensified, then stopped. Paramedics, county police and firemen swarmed into the wreckage of the clubhouse.

Sanchez wiped the sweat out of his eyes and shook his head to clear the fog. "Good timing," he said to the muscular young paramedic who stooped to relieve him of his knife and cut away his shirt. "Did Russ call you?"

"Nope," the man said. "Somebody named Pella."

"How in hell…?"

"She told the dispatcher she was using the phone in your truck." The man slapped a bandage over Hank's shoulder, tightened it and attached it with tape. "There, that'll hold you until we get to the hospital. Just sit there a minute while we load this guy. His legs may be broken." His cheerful grin belied the diagnosis. "Kinda strange, I think. Why doesn't the marshal of Chuparrosa carry his cell phone and his gun when he charges into a bombed out building?"

Chapter 19

Hank Sanchez sprawled half in and half out of the passenger side of his pickup, head against the backrest, the blood-soaked shirt draped over his bandaged shoulder. His eyes were fixed on the fire fighters as they squelched the final embers still flaring in hot, red bursts, sending sparks like celebrating stars into a solemn sky. A weaving of hoses draped the ground. They snaked among boxed trees and fallen boulders to the shell of the building, standing derelict, its form and energy altered.

County policemen and firemen gathered in clusters, checking each others' reactions to the explosion. Rhys Jones, who had sped out after he picked up the alarm on his radio, now circulated among them as the marshal's eyes and ears.

In the midst of the confusion, Russ had called from the gatehouse for help with the jittery citizens who were gathering there in worried groups to share whatever misinformation could be picked up from observation or rumor. One officer was sent down to urge everybody to go back home.

Pella sat silently on the driver's side of the pickup, her knuckles ten spots of white as she clung to the steering wheel. Her face was streaked with dust and the heel had been torn off one of her sandals. The uneven hem of her silk dress showed rips in two places. She didn't speak to Hank, though occasionally he was aware of her strained gray eyes studying him, as if she wondered who the hell this bloody stranger was.

Detective Jakobsen from the County Sheriff's Office, an intense young man with a receding hairline, peppered them with questions. He made it plain he didn't like their answers. Neither did Hank.

"You saw the person who shot you?" he asked for the third time.

"I saw two shadows." Breathing was getting to be an effort. He longed to lie down. "One of them shot me."

"Any better guess about the size of the gun?" His tone suggested that a competent lawman would have hung on to the bullet, instead of letting it exit his back.

"Too dark to see much. A handgun. I'm guessing a Colt 45, maybe. Did you check to see if Dingle's was missing?"

Jakobsen gave his head a gloomy shake. "Well, we'll come back in the morning with a metal detector. Dingle must have seen them. We'll question him as soon as he's conscious."

His assistant, carrying a slab of white plaster in a box, touched Jakobsen's shoulder. "We found a print. Looks like the one from the golf course vandalism."

Hank's head came up, and he squirmed forward for a look, ignoring the pain that shot through his right side. Only the pointed toe and narrow heel of the slim cowboy boot had left an impression on the plaster. Damn! He'd forgotten about Zephyr. "Rhys!" he shouted, his voice too thin to carry where he aimed it.

"I'll get him." Pella slipped out of the cab, limped in her disabled shoes to Jones's side and brought him back to the pickup.

"Rhys, go back to Zephyr's place right now and get her out of there." Hank pulled himself forward. "It's urgent."

Jones looked surprised. "I've been there twice tonight. She was fine when I saw her earlier. Jake hadn't even come home yet. What if she won't leave?"

Hank glanced at the detectives who had stepped away and lowered his voice to a whisper. "Arrest her. Tell her you have a warrant. But don't take her downtown." He tried to think beyond the pain. "Take her...take her to Fiesta's."

Rhys stared blankly at the marshal. "On what charge? You okay, Hank?"

"Just ask Fiesta to keep her until we can settle this. Call Charlie at the Miner's Delight. Get him to meet you there. If Jake is home, she'll be in trouble, and you could be, too. Get her out of there, man, any way you can."

Sanchez watched the deputy jog toward his patrol car, shuddering as a spasm shot through his disarrayed shoulder muscles again. He was covered with dust from the explosion and the dried blood on his chest tickled with every painful breath. Half an hour before, the paramedics had whisked Kevin Dingle off to the hospital, but the marshal managed to pull rank. Treatment at the Chuparrosa Emergency Clinic would be quicker. As long as the killer roamed the town, the marshal had to think about Saturday.

Jakobsen sauntered out of the darkness, a spruce contrast in his shirt and tie. "If you're headed to the ER, you better get going," he said, shaking his head. "The clinic's your choice, but it's a bad one. Have the wound cleaned out and get shots. You won't try to drive, will you?"

"I'm driving." Pella pulled herself up behind the steering wheel and started the ignition.

The detective shoved Hank's leaden feet into the car and slammed the door. They began winding their way between emergency vehicles and palo verde boxes to the paved road. His body recoiled with pain at each rut and bounce. It was better to talk than suffer in silence.

"So you ran to my truck and dialed 911?"

"It seemed like the most heroic thing to do." She flipped the words out, but her teeth were clenched, as if there were screams inside her fighting to be heard.

"I told you to stay hidden," he challenged, remembering what a terrorist with a gun could have done to her. He wouldn't have been able to stop him.

"Sure, and watch you...b-bleed to death." She gave a cough, denying the sob. Her eyes remained fixed on the far end of the headlights, as she perched on the edge of the seat and hunched over the steering wheel. Her feet in broken shoes had to stretch for the floor pedals.

"Sorry." Hank let his head roll back. "You've had a shock."

"Don't patronize me!"

He closed his eyes, contenting himself with the welcome sound of her honest anger.

The police had alerted the clinic. The physician on duty, Dr. Abdul Mohajur, his dark face slit by a row of white teeth, was waiting for them. He took an x-ray and cleaned the wound with gentle efficiency, assuring Hank, in careful English, that the bullet had only torn the muscles.

"Do you realize how lucky you are? A few inches over or down would have been extremely serious. It made a mess on the back, but by chance, missed all your bones. Doctor Mohajur sighed. "The man was a terrible shot."

Pella sat waiting, enclosed in her shell of tension, her face smudged and pale, uncertainty in her eyes.

"You'll be in some pain for awhile," the doctor explained, waving a packet of pills in front of him before handing them to Pella. "These will help you sleep." He made Hank swallow two on the spot.

"Do you mind driving me home?" Sanchez asked when they pushed through the clinic door into the soft warmth of the September midnight. The nursing attendant had cleaned him up a bit and given him a flannel sheet to replace the ruined shirt. A sling carried his arm and made his shoulder more comfortable. He had disposed of the shirt in the clinic's trash barrel.

Pella shrugged, dug into her purse for his keys, and watched, frowning, as he struggled into the truck's cab.

The moon had long ago sunk behind the western mountains. Except for headlights, the streets of Chuparrosa were lit only by occasional driveway reflectors and a few low-level yard lights. He wondered how many of the residents had been roused by the explosion and if some of them were still milling around the clubhouse. No inside lights were visible in the houses they passed, suggesting that their occupants were again dreaming of Saturday's parade.

Pella turned the pickup into the driveway of Hank's condo, switched off the motor and continued to grip the steering wheel.

"Come in for a few minutes, will you?" Hank asked, reaching across to the door handle with his left hand. "I have to call Rhys. He can take you home."

She removed the keys, slipped to the ground and crept like a sleepwalker toward the front door, holding it for him so he could enter before her. Then she followed him in, and he heard her shove it closed. There were two clunks as her sandals were kicked off onto the tiled floor. Puzzled, he halted his progress toward the wall phone in the galley kitchen, and turned carefully around to stare at her. In spite of the silky clinging of her dress, she looked like a waif, blond hair tousled, eyes huge, distraught.

He was hit by the sudden, queasy sensation that the walls of his condo were undulating downward in waves from ceiling to floor. He tossed off the sheet and grabbed the back of a chair with his free hand to steady himself.

Pella ducked her head, blond hair swinging in front of her eyes. "I'm going to stay here tonight, Hank. You need someone with you." When she looked up, Hank saw the hesitant plea for understanding in her face, all jumbled up with love and fear and need.

He took a deep unbelieving breath. She'd acted so cool all evening. "You like widowhood so much you're ready to risk a commitment with a cop?" His head was swimming. "Your timing's awful, *mi corazon.* I can barely stand up."

She bent in a graceful arc to collect her shoes and reached for the doorknob. Her head went up. "Then I'll walk home," she said.

It was a long way back to where she stood, four or five feet, at least. Hank breached the gap somehow and scooped her body against him with all the one-armed energy he could muster. She wanted sincerity? Well, she'd come to the right place. In a painful effort, he nudged her chin up and kissed her, tasting her tears, hoping that this time the fire he felt surging through her was only for him, that she wouldn't be pulling away again.

"I need you with me tonight and every night. Warm against me. In my heart. In my arms," he breathed in Spanish, shook his woozy head, and repeated the phrases in English, so she would have no doubt about his feelings.

With his left shoulder against the door, he clung to her. He didn't want to faint at her feet, but the lightheadedness was increasing. Since passion had never made him dizzy, he knew it was either the pain pill or the loss of blood, "*Querida,* there seem to be two of you, and I don't know which one to kiss. Do...do you think we could get to the sofa or—mm—the bedroom?"

A frazzled thread of hysteria ran through Pella's laugh. Stretching up she took his face in her hands. He felt her fingers run over its contours, touching the rough scar above his eyebrow—the reminder of another gunshot wound. Her tears had washed clean trails through the dust on her cheeks. The look in her eyes was a gift he had given up hoping to receive.

"I think you need someone to tuck you in," she said. Her arm around his waist, she guided him toward the hallway. Her other hand fumbled at the buttons on her dress.

The clock on Hank's darkened bedroom table said 6:15 when the throbbing in his shoulder, sharp and persistent, dragged him into consciousness. He lay still a moment, breathless with pain, wondering what he had done with the packet of pills Dr. Mujahur had given him. The bathroom, he guessed. Then remembering his wobbling head of the night before, he decided on a strong dose of aspirin instead. He rolled out, keeping his right side as still as possible.

"Where are you going?" Pella murmured.

He stopped mid-stride and turned to stare at her, startled and suddenly aware that he was naked. "A pill," he said and stumbled to the bathroom.

Minutes later he returned, watching her sleek head on his pillow, marveling that she was there at all. "You spent the night," he said. How could that longed-for event be such a blank in his mind?

"You passed out." Pella mumbled, her voice thick with sleep. "I thought you needed some undrugged person with you."

"I did." Wonder was replacing pain. He walked to her side of the bed and crawled under the sheet so he could lie on his left side, facing her. "I do. Are you at all interested in making love with a one-armed Hispanic?"

She nodded, and he felt a sensuous quiver.

"Good. Now listen to me. I've got to get this water business settled before our savage friend does any more damage." Sanchez eased his left arm under her head and tried to concentrate on being serious, terribly aware of her lying next to him in some thin satin wisps of undies, legs bare, shoulders bare, and best of all, willing. It was only with a great effort that he was able to force his groggy mind toward some plan of action. "Kevin is in the hospital, so we're shorthanded. Rhys and Gus will have to pick up the slack. I want you to stay with me or with Bent until we nab these guys." The need to convince her that he was serious made him frown. "I mean every minute."

The protest was forming on her lips, so he rolled his head over to her mouth and laid a long, slow kiss on it. "The festival parade," she whispered and gave a sob.

Not sure if it was the kiss or disappointment, he went on kissing her until the telephone shrilled. Pella stretched over him to pick it up and hold it to his ear.

"Hank!" Patsy Hagerty's whiney voice drilled into his ear. "Where are you and Pella? It's time to start lining up the parade!"

"We're on our way, Patsy." Sanchez heard his own voice and didn't recognize it . There weren't any words bad enough to describe the way he felt. "Ten minutes."

"When this is over," he said, his words slurred as he buried his face in Pella's neck, "you and I are going somewhere without phones and spend a week in bed." He heard Pella's forlorn sigh ripple behind him as he pushed himself upright and began searching for his clothes.

Chapter 20

At nine o'clock that night, Marshal Enrique Sanchez sat on his heels on the crest of a gravel mound, watching high-powered flashlights bob crazily across the blacked-out area below him. In this semi-darkness, Carlos and Jose Estavez, two-thirds of the Newcome Fireworks Company team, were beginning to insert the rockets that would soon blast from their metal casings to fill the desert night with radiance.

A horned moon hesitated high on the western edge of an inky sky. More illumination came from the brightly lit Sonoran Skyline Cochise Clubhouse behind him. Twenty-five yards from that open patio, a shallow trench held rocket tubes set in a sturdy frame. These, he had been told, were to be filled with the special multi-stage starburst rockets that would provide a spectacular up-close climax for the one hundred or so members and invited guests gathered there.

Five hours earlier, when Hank and Pella arrived, munching hotdogs, Ford Wheat had introduced them to Rusty Newcome, boss of the operation. Sanchez squinted at the man as they shook hands in the light of the disappearing afternoon sun. All day he had been focused on the search for steely turquoise eyes, but the ones peering out from under the brim of Newcome's cap, were dark brown and hinted at a sense of humor. Faded red hair curled over his ears. Fortyish and thick-bodied, he guided his two Hispanic helpers from the seat of a motorized wheelchair with studded tires. No disguised Isaiah Morley there.

"We'll burn a hundred rockets, Marshal. And that's a hell of a lot of gun powder," Newcome boasted to Hank and Pella. "We start with a

166

few bombs. Then we'll go into the knockout stuff. Chrysanthemums, palm trees, comets. This was a last minute order and a short twenty minute program, so tonight we'll just do it the old-fashioned way. We'll touch 'em off with lighting sticks." He waved a hand at the trucks behind him. "We got tons of fireworks and equipment to unload and organize before then. I gotta get the boys started. It takes me a mite longer than some folks."

He had jolted away across the scraped desert ground toward the trucks, calling over his shoulder, "Went off a highway bridge on my Harley two years ago. One last exciting ride."

Ford Wheat, his fingers a bracelet circling Packy's listless wrist, had stood with Carlos and Jose as they unloaded lumber, shovels and other paraphernalia from the trucks. His good-natured face was disfigured by a deep frown of preoccupation. Once he glanced at the marshal's shoulder. "I heard you got shot."

Sanchez nodded and said, "It's okay." He'd been telling people that lie all day. It ended the conversation and hid the fact that he was tired as the devil and the pain never let up, in spite of the aspirin he'd been popping every few hours. He'd found the wound didn't hurt any worse if he pitched the sling and kept his hand in his pocket, so except for a bulge of bandage under his shirt, his injury didn't show. And he avoided some of the questions.

Pella had been with him part of the day, from the cool dawn hours when they'd lined up the parade and started the wild kaleidoscope of people, horses, bikes, floats and marching bands on its triumphant journey down Gold Dust Road. Later on they'd taken endless foot tours through the closed off streets of downtown Chuparrosa, where throngs of visitors munched pizza and hotdogs and sipped wine, while they scanned the arts and crafts displayed in the booths, and tapped their feet to the music of the brass oompah band on the plaza.

Sanchez had turned Pella lose for the Old Settlers' Luncheon, under the watchful eye of Tyler Bent, while he cruised the rest of the town. Then he'd taken a gravel road outside the city limits to tour the rodeo grounds. After the calf roping started, he tracked down Charlie Talaferro, who was manning the announcer's booth above the dusty arena. The man appeared even more dangerous than usual, with an oversized six-shooter in a holster hanging from the belt buckled around his waist. He grinned and advised Hank not to worry.

"Nothin's going to happen out here on my watch!" he promised, slapping the gun. "I'll catch up with you later, in case you need me."

On the way back to Chuparrosa, Hank swung up Buckskin Road to look in on the pickets, and groaned when he saw the KEEZ television trucks with gaudy red "keys" painted on their sides. A crowd of bystanders was lined up across the road on the Sonoran Skyline side to watch the show. Teams of men with cameras and microphones were setting up shop and circulating among the pickets. There seemed to be a lot of interviewing going on. In the middle of the throng of picketers, Micah and Jeremiah Morley stood with their heads together bending over the interviewer's mike. Near the road, Sugar was gesturing toward Isaiah's signs, the scowl on her face betraying her bitter intensity, as she spoke to another mike-holder.

Fiesta, her gold cowboy hat set at a saucy angle, threw back her head with a howl of delight when she noticed the marshal's patrol car idling in the road and came swooping down on him, dragging one of the reporters by the arm.

"Marshal, darling, your timing is magical," she trilled. "Here's Vic North to catch every golden word about your version of Chuparrosa's empty spigot."

Sanchez gave her a black look and shook hands with the reporter. He wasn't going to get out of his patrol car. With luck the guy would get tired of leaning on the window with the sun searing his face, and go away.

"Ask him to tell you about the Roger Martineau's murder," Fiesta cooed in Vic's ear, tipping her hat forward to shield her eyes from the glare.

"Sorry, Vic, that's an ongoing investigation," Sanchez drawled, falling back on an age-old excuse. "It'll be a few days before we can talk about it, and then I'd suggest you contact the county people. They'll have more details than I will." Vic opened his mouth, but the marshal cut him off. "What I'm really concerned about just now is preventing you and all the folks gathered here from becoming victims of heat stroke. You may have noticed there's not much shade. Have you got plenty of water? Keeping all these people hydrated is of first importance. In fact I'm going to hustle back downtown right now to arrange a delivery of several cases of bottled water and bags of ice. If you'll excuse me…"

Hank accelerated, forcing the startled reporter to shut his mouth and jump back. Fiesta shook her fist at him as he spun the patrol car around and sped toward the busy heart of Chuparrosa. He could tell from her face that she was screaming "coward."

At the gas station on West Gold Dust Road, Sanchez told the owner to put the water and ice on the town's tab, and a couple of teenagers, lounging around the candy bar shelves, were appointed to deliver them to the picketers.

The sun was resting on the pinnacle of the St. Jude's Thumb by the time he went looking for Pella. The afternoon crowd, milling around the craft stalls, had thinned this late in the day, but a few shoppers still searched for bargains as the vendors began to pack up their wares. He caught sight of her at last sitting on a bench in the shade of a mesquite tree with Tyler Bent. They were licking ice cream cones. He steered the patrol car into a no parking zone and strolled over to join them.

"Is that dinner?" Hank asked.

"We were too hungry to make a decision about dinner," Pella said. "So we're having dessert before we cruise the food booths." A laugh tumbled out through the pale exhaustion on her face. "Are you all right?"

"Sure. Do you have to stay here while the vendors take down their booths?"

"Hey, how's your shoulder, man?" Tyler cut in. "I'm about to take off for the pageant. You want Pella to come with me?"

"Pella can speak for herself," she said firmly to both men. "If we can get Rhys to take over here for awhile, I should go to Sonoran Skyline to oversee the fireworks setup."

They'd bought hot dogs and chips and driven back past the picket lines to the fireworks site. There, Pella kept going through her paces, concern darkening her eyes every time she looked Hank's way. When Charlie Talaferro stopped by after dark, still wearing his fancy cowboy getup, the six-shooter in its holster, Hank persuaded her to go with the big man to the pageant at the school gym.

"This'll be dull duty until it's time to light the fuses," he'd said. "Go check on Maude. Charlie'll make sure you get back before the blast-off." He could tell from the man's grim nod that he understood it was the changing of the guard.

It had been dull. And tense. Just standing around wondering why Wheat stared at him, his eyes narrowed with distrust, and why Packy's head swiveled on its delicate stem so that the marshal was always in his line of vision. The boy even managed to stumble backwards when his grandfather stalked after Rusty's wheel chair. Wheat never let go of the child's wrist, and Packy didn't struggle to get away, but the eyes in his pinched face fastened on Sanchez like the puff grass seeds clinging to the hem of his oversized jeans.

Wheat and the child had driven away in the Rolls about the time the stars came out. Hank knew they'd returned after an hour or so, Wheat in a fresh shirt and Packy sucking a grape popsicle. Now they were down talking to Rusty.

Sanchez stood up on the mound to stretch his legs. Digging the shallow trenches and constructing two sets of rocket frames, a long one for the center of the cleared area, a shorter one nearer the clubhouse, had occupied the team's hours before the sun disappeared leaving a pink rim on the western mountains. By the time Jose hammered the final nails into the rough boards, and the depot boxes of shells had been wheeled into place, the palm trees at the clubhouse were ebony silhouettes against a cloudless night sky. Carlos and Jose, with miners' lights on their hard hats, would handle the loading. Rusty, who had turned on the running lights fastened to the arms of his chair, would torch the fuses. Stationary floods, low on the ground, were ready to be flicked on just before the show began.

Newcome had taken pains to demonstrate the flares used to light the rockets, as well as the crew's fire extinguishers, drum of water and first aid kit. "No need to get excited, Marshal. We set off shows with these light sticks for years before electronics came along," he said. "Lots more fun than pushing buttons. We have to be extra careful in dry Arizona, but our company's been doin' this since the end of World War II, and we've never started a fire."

The three men pulled fireproof jumpsuits over their clothes. Newcome passed out extra hard hats for the marshal and his deputies. There seemed to be nothing wrong with the operation. It was as tight and official as the county licenses Ford had given him days before.

Sanchez rubbed his forehead. The aspirin made his ears ring. He worked his shoulder, trying to get the lacerated muscles into a more comfortable position. He managed to tune them, instead, to an irritated pitch. The damn thing was just going to torment him.

Sounds of music and laughter drifted toward Hank from the patio of the Sonoran Skyline Clubhouse. A lighthearted, civilized hum. Members and friends, the privileged few, were settling into lawn chairs or milling around with their cocktails. Every time the doors of the clubhouse opened, he caught the aroma of steak and barbeque, a pungent stab to his empty belly. It had been five hours since the lone hotdog.

On the field below a lantern was lifted, and the light flashed briefly on Pella's bright head. Charlie, his arm around her, was talking to Rhys Jones and Gus Kremer. Hank turned on his own flashlight to find his way to them across the stony patch of desert.

"How do you want to do this, Hank? Where do you want us?" Gus Kremer called, when the marshal got close enough to hear. "It's gonna be mighty thin without Kevin."

For the last two days, Sanchez had begged Lubeck for the emergency loan of a couple county patrolmen. But, between cutbacks and gang-bangers, the county had its own problems. Friday night Lubeck had called to say that there weren't any men available, unless Chuparrosa wanted to hire them off-duty. So as a last resort, Hank had run the issue past Mayor Bergen. The mayor bristled at the idea and shot down any suggestion of renting outside help. Then he accused his marshal of paranoia. Ford Wheat, he hissed, was a civic-minded gentleman who would do everything by the book, and Chuparrosa was going to give him the honor of trusting him. Knowing his man, Hank figured his uneasy intuition had no chance of winning in a battle with Bergen's esteem for Wheat.

"Maybe Charlie…," Kremer suggested. Sanchez shook his head, and the deputy shrugged.

"I want you two on the perimeter of the firing area, one going one way and one the other. The patrol line will circle between the clubhouse on the west and the road on the east. You're acting as a fence to keep out anyone except the people you see here now. I'll do the same from an inside circle. Watch me, in case I need you. Keep your shoulder radios live."

They trotted off in opposite directions, as Rusty Newcome lit his first flare, and in the glow, Sanchez could see Ford Wheat, holding Packy in his arms, standing beside the frame of aerial bombs due to be set off. What kind of a *pinché fallon* would risk his grandchild like that, Hank wondered?

"I want you and Charlie to go over to the road," he said to Pella. "Fireworks scatter a lot of litter. You might be hit or burned." He took the hard hat from under his arm, settled it on his head and passed his broad brimmed straw to her. "Will you hold this for me?"

"I'll try not to singe your hat, but I'm staying here." Her chin was up as she balanced the hat on the back of her head. Her eyes dared him to order her away.

"We'll stand under those palo verdes." Charlie nodded at the boxed trees a hundred feet from the trenches. "What about the kid?"

"I'm going to get him now."

Packy was asleep on Wheat's shoulder and mumbled incoherently when Hank scooped him onto his left arm. The effort to lift the child made him grit his teeth.

"This is completely unnecessary," Wheat protested, struggling to retain his hold on Packy. "He'll be safer with me."

"He'll be with you, Mr. Wheat, but you'll have to watch from the sidelines."

A breeze brushed the child's hair from his forehead. His eyes were closed, but he fastened his arms around Hank's neck like a clamp. Off to the northwest, came the cry of a single coyote, an eerie yapping that ended in a wild, gleeful howl. Even in the dim light of the flare, Hank could see a subtle change on the other man's face. The domineering tone gave way to compliance.

"Ah, yes." Wheat's chuckle sounded forced. "Under the tree with Pella and Talaferro? Good idea." He stepped out in that direction.

Charlie has a gun, Hank thought, as he bent to pass the sleeping child to Pella. He better know how to use it.

The first salute cracked skyward as he headed toward the firing site, and he heard Packy's waking shrieks of terror. He jogged over the open space while more bombs exploded, reverberating above him, echoing off the near mountains. Packy screamed on.

The team of men worked swiftly in the haze of acrid smoke, touching the fuses one at a time and reloading the empty mortars from the covered depot box. Burning fragments of debris sifted onto Hank's shirt.

"Hope you're wearin' cotton, Marshal," Rusty boomed from his wheel chair through a megaphone. He touched his torch to another rocket and sent it streaking toward the stars. "Polyester'll melt and burn ya' bad. Cover your ears. Here comes a big one."

Directly overhead the big one burst into thunder that shot through Hank's shoulder like a bolt of lightning. Shaken, he paused to take a breath in the stench of sulfur and noise. Lights guiding the deputies' feet revolved like planets around the firing zone. Sanchez chose a loop closer in, careful to avoid the wooden frames of the mortar boxes. As the rockets whooshed to the heavens, he paced the route, searching the darkness for the dancing shadow. He was sure now the howling coyote would turn up. All his remaining strength would be hoarded for that rendezvous.

Ten minutes into the display, Sanchez passed the mound in front of the clubhouse. The two-inch trench and scaffolding held the end-of-show fancy rockets that were waiting for Newcome's flame. Lights silhouetted the crowd of members and their friends o-o-oing from the patio. He hiked down the north side of the area and swung past the masses of people lining the road on the east. A collective "Ah-h-h!"

rose from their throats as a blue and gold chrysanthemum spread out and twinkled, eclipsing the stars.

Rhys Jones appeared along the fence, doing his unbalanced jog past the upturned faces. He circled his light to signal all was well and vanished into the darkness.

From the center of the smoky maelstrom, Sanchez could hear Newcome shouting orders, but the trio's figures were indistinct. Or were there four bodies in that fiery furnace? He slapped at a burning fragment of paper casing that scorched his hand, realizing how easy it was going to be for someone to slip between him and the deputies and hide in the camouflage of that evil-smelling inferno.

As an enormous palm tree rocket climbed toward the zenith, glittering in green and gold, Sanchez ducked into the haze to count the occupants. The hiss and whoosh of rockets pounded on his ears, and he blinked fumes out of his eyes. Carlos and Jose didn't glance up from their work. Newcome, his face blackened and streaked with sweat, flourished the flare toward the next fuse. There were still three men. Only three.

"Twelve more shots 'n then we head up the hill," Newcome shouted and grinned at Hank. "Those are really bee-uti-ful."

The mound. Of course. The mound! So easy to get there over the golf course. All those people were lined up like targets on the clubhouse patio. Rockets loaded, fuses laid out like cat's tails. Sanchez began to sprint across the desert. Loose sand caught at his boots as he dodged prickly pear and cholla, picked out by his flashlight beam. Ahead of him the obsidian curve of the low hill stood out against a sheen of clubhouse lights. And on it moved a furtive shadow.

A flame shot quickly across the fuses the length of the bunker. The figure kicked violently, again and again, at the frame in the shallow trench that held the mortars, tipping it over toward the patio. Then he whirled back to make his escape. In the next moment Sanchez was there, vaulting over the last few feet to hurl himself on the moving wraith. He caught him just above the knees, his heavy plastic helmet butting the man in the small of his back. The fuses reached the lifting charge and the rockets exploded from their mortars, roaring toward the clubhouse patio.

Sanchez gasped for breath. The agony of contact with a hard body shuddered through his damaged muscles. They sprawled on the ground, Hank taller, heavier, but the other man wriggling like a snake, slipping out of his grasp.

"Settle down, *viboro* " Sanchez ordered. "You're not going anywhere."

The earth shook with the vibrations of rockets, as they scooted sideways, just off the ground. Sulfur fumes surrounded them. From the patio came shrieks of agony and fear interspersed with the fizz and roar, then the sound of shattering glass.

"Bulls-eye!" the man shouted and gave a coyote howl. In a twist of effort he squirmed away, and for an instant, by the light from the burning clubhouse, Hank saw the turquoise eyes mocking him. The man bounced to his feet like a dancer. A quick kick sent the toe of his boot smashing into the marshal's right shoulder.

Hank's bellow of fury became a battle cry to keep from passing out. He staggered upright and launched himself at the legs that were vanishing into the night, catching them low, just above the ankles. The man dropped heavily on a downhill slope, grunting as he landed.

Once more they grappled on the granite chips, Sanchez aware of blood from his shoulder oozing through the bandage onto his shirt, running down his arm. He clung to the man, waiting for a chance to grab his gun, screaming into his radio. What in hell had happened to his deputies?

"Let him go, Marshal." The voice was whispery, poisonous. Hank felt the cold, stubby barrel of the Derringer Wheat pressed against his temple.

"You going to shoot me, Wheat?" Sanchez wheezed out, stalling for time. The feet he was restraining came alive, landing blows to his body.

"No, I'm going to let Isaiah Morley do it." Wheat gestured to the man on the ground. "Stand up, Izzy!"

"My deputies..." The words came hard, breathy.

"All gone to help the poor people in the fire. Don't worry, Marshal. You're going down bravely in the line of duty, shot to death by an escaping convict."

"Don't call me a convict, you corrupt son of a bitch." A derisive growl came out of the darkness from the other man. "I'm savin' the earth. You're stealin' a company."

"Corrupt? I bought and paid for you, Morley. You were for sale, and I was the only bidder." Wheat glanced over his shoulder. Lights were bobbing through the haze of smoke hanging over the firing site. "Newcome's coming this way. Finish the job, you no good twit, and get out of here. I've got a fire to put out."

Gathering his strength, Sanchez pushed himself into a crouching position. Behind him, he could hear screams and yelling, while in the distance came the wail of fire trucks. The other two men stood up, but he stayed low to the ground, ready to grab at any chance that might come.

Isaiah Morley's hand hesitated as he reached for the .45 in his belt. "I've got enough on my head," he snapped. "Save your own damn development."

"Your walking papers are right here, all the cash you'll need," Wheat screamed over the noise of the emergency vehicles tearing to the scene. He patted his breast pocket. "You can fly to Mexico and be free and clear, if you get rid of him."

The .45 came out of Morley's belt. In a split second Sanchez knew his chances were better with the less accurate Derringer. As the barrel came up, he uncoiled back at Morley's legs, grabbing his knees, sending him sprawling, spinning with him down the incline into the shadows. He counted two shots from Wheat's gun. The first whizzed too close to his ear. The next grazed his boot. He had ten seconds to get that .45 away from Morley before Wheat reloaded. Scrambling like a wildcat, Hank swung out with his flashlight, catching the side of the man's head with a satisfying crunch. The turquoise eyes flashed in surprise before the lids slumped over them.

"Drop it, Mr. Wheat."

It was Pella's voice, clear and determined. Sanchez stuck the .45 in his belt and cuffed Isaiah's hands together before he looked up. She stood, feet apart, in a straight arm pose, a revolver pointed at Wheat's bald head.

"Now, Mr. Wheat."

Hank heard the metallic snap of Pella's gun being cocked.

"Pella, my dear, don't be foolish." Wheat attempted a chuckle, his hands busy with the Derringer. "You aren't going to shoot an old friend. Sanchez and I just caught the culprit of all these deeds."

"Pella seems determined to shoot you, Ford." Sanchez stumbled to his feet. "Better drop the gun."

Impotent fury washed over Wheat's face. His fingers opened. The Derringer and the two bullets he was trying to load into it struck the gravel.

"Hank! A-are you all right?" Pella called, gun still raised. She looked fearless, but her voice shook.

Sanchez floundered out from the shadows, aware that the right side of his shirt was soaked with blood. He felt older than time. He glared at the back of Milford Wheat's head as he read him his rights and snapped on handcuffs.

"How did you get that gun away from Charlie?" he asked Pella.

"I stole it. Wheat said you'd be at the fire, but I couldn't find you." She stared at him, then finally lowered the revolver, her control seeping away. "My God, look at you!"

"Did you release the hammer?" Gently he took the weapon out of her hands, checked it and rotated out the cylinder. "It's—umm—not loaded, Pella."

She put her hands over her face and began to weep. "Oh, thank God," she said.

Chapter 21

Kevin Dingle blinked and opened his eyes to the world again four days after the disastrous Chuparrosa fireworks display.

His mother, who had been sitting by his hospital bed ever since he'd arrived smashed and bloody, burst into grateful tears. Nurses and doctors were summoned and clustered around, making the necessary adjustments to his treatment, while Mrs. Dingle, still dabbing her eyes, stepped out into the hall to phone the good news to his dad and the rest of the family.

Kevin scowled at the cast that enveloped his left leg, fingered his bandaged head and, feeling less immortal than ever before in all his twenty-one years, meditated in silent wonder on how close he'd come to not waking up at all.

Lunch, Jell-o and a bowl of broth with a few grains of rice lurking at the bottom, depressed him still more, but he perked up when Rhys Jones stuck his head in the room and asked, "Are you ready for company?"

"Damn right I am." He pushed the button that cranked the bed up a couple of notches. "What damn luck to miss the excitement you guys stirred up at Sonoran Skyline."

"Oh yeah, we've been busy." Rhys settled himself in the guest chair by Dingle's bed, pulled out a notebook and surveyed his cast and bandages. "Do you remember anything about Friday night? I heard you got yourself pretty badly knocked around."

Kevin squirmed to relieve an itch in his cast. "I thought you guys would have that all figured out."

"I'm supposed to get a statement from you about what you saw and heard before the bomb went off at the clubhouse construction site. Have the county attorney and Sergeant Lubeck been to see you yet? No? Reporters?" He chuckled. "We're gonna make you a celebrity, kid."

Fame had a strong appeal for Kevin, so he tried to concentrate, to creep through the fog hanging over his mind. "I remember walking around the building that night with my flashlight on." Stumped, he paused to think again. "I guess the outside lights went off. Yeah, and I decided to call the gate for backup before I went to investigate."

"What did you see or hear?"

Dingle pleated the sheet between his fingers and shook his head. "Nothing. Nothing. It was damn quiet. I didn't get far either. I-I guess they hit me when I came out of the entrance to make the call." Not a proud record. It occurred to him that he might not get paid for that night. After all, he'd let a bomb go off in the building while on duty as guard. Greenwood Development wasn't likely to send him flowers. He wondered if they could sue him for messing up.

"Don't feel bad. If you'd seen 'em, they might have shot you on the spot."

"Oh. Yeah," Kevin said, not feeling cheered.

"At least they dragged you out of the way of the bomb. The marshal found you trussed up in a back corner. They took your gun, by the way."

"Oh, swell!" Kevin closed his eyes and made a valiant effort to summon up more scraps of memory – scents, sounds, feelings. He drew a blank. After the floodlights went out, he'd crept to the front entrance by his flashlight's glow, and the next five days had been washed away in a dark sea. He suddenly recalled a date he'd had with Glory Windom for Sunday afternoon. They'd planned to go fishing out on the Verde. It seems he'd stood her up. Another black mark.

"What fell on my legs?"

"Burning scaffolding. Want me to sign your cast? You're lucky, boy, that you don't have one on each leg."

Kevin said, "Yeah, I guess so." His mind still chewed the notion that he'd probably lost his girl, and Greenwood Development would take him to court. "When did the marshal get there?"

"Just before the bomb went off. He started to chase them and took a bullet in the shoulder. From your .45. Then he went in and cut you loose."

"Wait! Go back." Dingle demanded. "Is the marshal okay?"

"Rhys shrugged and began doodling on his pad. "He'd have been a hellava lot better," he muttered, "if he hadn't had that fight with Morley on Saturday night."

"Isaiah?" Kevin grinned. So he'd been right about one thing at least. "Isaiah blew up my clubhouse and shot the marshal? Wow!"

Jones looked down at his note pad and scratched his head. "And the next night Isaiah messed with the fireworks. When the rockets hit that clubhouse, Ford Wheat hailed Gus and me and told us to meet Hank up there to help the people on the patio who were hurt. It seemed like the right thing to do, what with people screaming and the clubhouse on fire. We didn't know Hank was at the firing site mixing it up with Morley."

"Rockets hit the clubhouse? The other clubhouse?" He squinted at Rhys sensing the man was confessing to an error in judgment that still bothered him. "Was anybody hurt?"

"Most of the people on the patio. A couple of women are still hospitalized with severe burns. Their clothes caught on fire. Eighteen were treated and released. Greenwood Development is cleaning up the damage and getting ready to deal with the lawsuits."

"Then it sounds like Mr. Wheat gave you good advice."

Rhys shifted in the plastic chair and frowned. "It was a diversion. Wheat had planned it with Morley. His damned advice nearly got Hank killed."

"Mr. Wheat's been working with Isaiah Morley?" Surprise made Dingle's voice rise to a squeak.

"He orchestrated this whole affair as the inside man. He wanted a local business to play with in his retirement. He knew Greenwood Development was financially shaky, but they refused to sell out so he could add Sonoran Skyline to his holdings. He decided to polish 'em off and pick 'em up when they went bankrupt. According to the FBI, he's played these ruthless tricks before, usually overseas, but they've never been able to catch him at it."

"But Mr. Wheat? Jeeze, he plays golf with the mayor."

"And the mayor is sure lookin' sheepish these days. Wheat decided he'd hire a local boy, an out-of-work eco-terrorist, trained in commando tactics, to do his dirty work."

"That's dumb. Isaiah wants to keep the desert natural, not tear it up for golf courses."

"True enough. And Wheat convinced him that destroying Sonoran Skyline would further the cause. For Isaiah it was a righteous one, even more true because of the water problems on his parent's place. Wheat didn't mention that he was planning to build a higher density development out there after Morley'd done his worst."

"So Wheat kept Isaiah supplied with all the information he needed?"

"Wheat palmed a key so he could reprogram the golf course computers and have the sprinklers to go off during the tournament. He knew which greens to tear up and where the irrigation connections were. He tried to scare off Hank by having Isaiah terrorize Pella..." Jones ticked them off on his fingers.

"Isaiah killed Roger Marineau?" Kevin tried to put that in perspective. He'd never known a murderer. Now a guy from his childhood, a guy who'd played with his brothers, who'd had the same teachers and sat in the same seats in high school was a murderer. He chewed his lip. That would take some getting used to.

"Well, Wheat claims he had nothing to do with the murder. When Isaiah finally tumbled to the fact that Wheat wasn't going to restore the desert and stop pumping water at Sonoran Skyline, he blew a fuse. Wheat thought he could hold him in line by threatening to turn him in and involve his whole family in the crimes. But Morley couldn't be intimidated so easily. He decided to bring down Wheat's empire by acting on his own. The messages he left were Bible references he used to justify his crimes. Wheat isn't troubled by any scruples, but he insists he didn't authorize Martineau's murder. When he found out he'd lost control of his eco-warrior, he was furious. Isaiah refused to go quietly, but Wheat knew Greenwood was about to fold. He thought he could still pull it off if they got rid of the marshal who knew too much."

"Hank figured this out?" Kevin shifted his weight, dropping his good leg over the edge of the bed. He was always amazed at how clearly the marshal could read people and events.

"Pella had found some clues to Greenwood's financial health in their files and the marshal began to have suspicions about Wheat's character. Greenwood admitted that they'd been approached by lawyers to sell the Skyline, but Wheat had been careful to keep his name out of the deal. You know how chary Hank is about probable cause. Chuparrosa isn't going to be embarrassed by a false arrest while he's around. He couldn't get the proof he needed until Wheat and Morely goofed up."

"Did Wheat ride with Isaiah on those greens?" The ridiculous vision of that plump little man as the phantom horseman galloped across his mind. Kevin stifled a grin and flexed his toes protruding from the lower end of the cast.

"No. Zephyr Wilson. Every time Jake beat her up, she'd run to Sugar for sympathy. Isaiah'd been camping down in the far reaches of the forest, but he loved his momma's meals. When he met Zephyr, he recognized a woman longing to be manipulated." The deputy shook his shaggy head. "I guess she was ripe to hook up with another man, too, but she picked the wrong one again. Isaiah talked her into a couple of capers. After they blew up the new clubhouse with you in it, the marshal had me take her to Fiesta's so Jake wouldn't kill her. Jake didn't care diddly about the clubhouse, but he couldn't have his woman messin' around with Isaiah."

"Is she goin' to jail?"

"She should get off lightly as the state's star witness."

"And Sugar? Butch? The boys?"

Rhys resumed the doodling on his notebook, his face sober. "They knew Isaiah'd violated his parole. They're in a bunch of trouble for hidin' him. Sugar let her son take her horses and trailer to destroy the greens. It doesn't look good."

Kevin frowned and stared out the window. The Morelys had been on Spanish Saddle Mountain since before he was born. If their well hadn't gone dry, they might not have let Isaiah back into their lives.

"Say, Kevin, remember that little kid, Packy? He belongs to some family in Brooklyn, New York, who sold him to Wheat. That was part of the solid citizen disguise Wheat thought he needed to play golf with the well-heeled residents in a small town. He's never had any children, never been married."

"That didn't look right to me. The kid's clothes were too big."

"He says his name's Josef. I hear they may ship him back to the coast, but not to his most lovin' family." Jones scratched his nose. "In the meantime, Hank asked Fiesta to keep Josef, too. That woman's a sucker for strays."

Kevin stared at the foot of his bed, thinking about his mom's tears of joy when he came out of the coma earlier in the day. How did a betrayed six-year-old cope with life, he wondered?

"Last night," Rhys reported, "the city council voted to put in a water line to Spanish Saddle Mountain. They'll have to get a bond issue passed. We'll vote on it next month. Until it's finished, they'll subsidize the tanks and water being trucked in for people whose wells have gone dry. Greenwood Development is restructuring and putting in a pipeline to bring effluent from the valley to water the courses. They've formed a Chuparrosa citizens group to advise them on desert sensitivity.

"You know the stone circle along Devil's Eye Creek?" the deputy rattled on. "Well, it's going back. A few of the stones were damaged when Isaiah blew up the clubhouse, but they'll cement 'em together. It'll be part of a permanent bird sanctuary. Of course Agatha's tellin' everybody she saw it in the smoke."

Dingle closed his eyes and rubbed his fingers across the strip of forehead sticking out beneath his bandage. He'd been out of it for only five days, but the world had taken a lot of turns since Friday. A childhood acquaintance had landed in jail for murder and a rich man, as old as his grandfather, had turned out to be a hoodlum. Agatha wasn't as crazy as he'd thought. Some of the absolutes in his life were clattering down around him. He needed to get back to work. How was he going to fit the cast into the patrol car? At least he could work nights on dispatch.

"When's the marshal comin' to see me? I'll likely be out of here and back on patrol in a couple days."

A nurse rustled in to poke a thermometer in his ear and then lift his wrist while she stared at her watch. A smile of skeptical amusement flitted across her face, but she didn't disagree with him.

"Hank's out of town." Jones flipped his notebook closed, replaced the pen in his shirt pocket and rose to go.

"Don't talk," the nurse told Kevin, without looking up. "I'll be through in a minute."

"Where?" he mouthed. Hank never went anywhere. Well, once he'd gone back to New Mexico for his sister's wedding. Just for the weekend. If he'd been shot why wasn't he in the hospital? He watched the nurse as she dropped his wrist, made some notes and marched off to her next patient.

"North Rim."

Dingle's eyes widened in disbelief. The North Rim of the Grand Canyon was a cold place this time of year. Another week and they'd close it until the middle of May. Unless you hiked down into the canyon where it was warmer, there was nothing to do. "God! Why? You said he got hurt."

"He got pretty well chewed up arresting Isaiah," Rhys agreed. "He stayed in the hospital over night so the doctors could do some repair work. The next day he came limping into the office and told me to take over for a week while he went to the North Rim. A little R and R." He chuckled. "That stands for revelry and romance."

"Huh?"

A broad grin softened the deputy's face. "Yeah. Seemed like he was in an awful hurry, too. He took Pella with him. Said something about not wantin' to give her a chance to change her mind."

Another absolute dropped with a thud. Kevin's image of the marshal as a cool loner made an abrupt shift to a hotheaded guy with unruly appetites. "But the North Rim...They don't have telephones or TVs in those cabins. And it's damn cold up there this time of year."

"That's right. Lots of freedom, though. And privacy. And time to do whatever they want to do." Rhys had a distant look in his eye as he strolled to the door. "I'll bet they'll find plenty of ways to keep warm."

"Would you introduce me to Agatha Purestone when we get back?"

Hank Sanchez looked at Pella VanDoren and laughed. He'd been laughing a lot during the past forty-eight hours. Ever since they'd arrived at the cabin on the North Rim. In fact, ever since they'd left Chuparrosa for the long drive north. "I'll be happy to do that," he said. "But why?"

"You see," Pella said, her eyes studying aspen leaves quaking above her head, "I think she is a really smart lady. She knew what was going on before anyone. She knew when to work on a solution and when to fade back to let things work on themselves."

"Not fair," he protested. "Isaiah was filling her in on all the details. She should be cited for not reporting it to the police."

The two of them had been walking since breakfast through the crisp, dry air of a high country morning. Between the trees on their left, they could catch glimpses of the Grand Canyon, a breathtaking gorge plunging through eons of rock strata down to the Colorado River. Now, at noon, the sunshine hung warm around their shoulders. They had shed their jackets and tied them around their waists. Boots made no sounds on the plateau rim trail, spongy with ancient layers of needles from the pine trees towering overhead. Birdsong had melted away. The aspens' sad black eyes stared into the distance from white trunks, and a breeze fluttered the few yellow leaves still clinging to the branches.

"Can you prove she knew his plans beforehand? No, of course you can't. They were old friends so he reassured her that he would tackle her problems. She saw he was a man on a mission, and she didn't question him. Smart lady."

"I don't think much of his mission or his methods," Hank growled. "He is a terrorist, Pella, killing innocent people to force his own way, and civilians be damned. Thank God he's locked up."

She cocked her head at him. "The water's running again on Spanish Saddle Mountain."

"You mean they're trucking water up the mountain. Well, the council would have gotten around to that." Sanchez was surprised to find himself an apologist for the Chuparrosa city council. "The town would have worked something out," he offered lamely.

"But think of the mess. This is almost clean and tidy compared to the lawsuits, the bankruptcies, angry citizens, a divided town – perhaps for years and years. How long would the mayor and the council have put off those hard decisions?"

He grinned at her earnest face. "You little *terrorista*. You're dangerous. I'm going to have to run you in. Maybe Greenwood can put off the bankruptcy, but you may be sure there'll be lawsuits and angry citizens to hell and back."

"But one thing is solved. You, bold defender of the right, have saved the town. Chuparrosa isn't going to dry up."

He hesitated. He wasn't going to lie to her. "There's still water under the ground, and they hope to find some way to recharge that aquifer. If the level can be raised, the creek will run again, and the springs might start flowing. That's the theory, anyway. The effluent from the valley towns will be processed to use on the golf courses, but all those pipes have to be laid underground, and they haven't dug the first trench." He shrugged. "Maybe we'll have torrential rains this winter."

"Yeh, right. Is that the best you can do?"

"No. The best we can do is to remember this is a desert. We've overburdened it with people and our civilized requirements for irrigation. Now we've got to live with the water we have and leave the rest of the watershed alone."

Pella slipped her hand in Hank's as they walked together, comfortable and at peace with one another, weariness and passion put aside for the moment. Memories of the fiery night and the ache of bitter battles were breaking up into vaporous bits, dissipating in the stillness of the woods. It was a relief to be shed of them, to be two normal people again.

"At least Isaiah got everyone's attention," she said, at last.

"True, I'll grant him that. Chuparrosa and the whole valley have put a clean white Band-aid on the problem and consider it solved. They won't worry about it again until the next development runs out of water, and they have to find another Band-aid."

"Let's hope it doesn't create another Isaiah. As I remember, that bastard wanted to kill you as well." She stopped to throw her arms around him and rest her face on his chest. "How's your shoulder today? You've been giving it some exercise lately."

Hank joined in the hug and let his hands wander. "You're the glue that's holding me together, *amante.*"

"Now that's a charming metaphor," Pella said, laughing. "So everything is handled, and we don't have to go back to work yet?"

"Just to the cabin, *querida.* Just for a rest." He kissed her, urgently. "Are you ready to turn around?"

She took her time, grinning, teasing him, her face lit by the sun. Then she reached for his hand. "Race ya'," she said.

Printed in the United States
74530LV00002BA/1-99